THE

TUESDAY NIGHT

KILLER

I AM A LOCAL WRITER SELF-PUBLISHING MY BOOKS.

IF YOU LIKE THIS BOOK YOU CAN ORDER MORE @ AMAZON OR CONTACT ME ON FACEBOOK.

ENJOY.

JAMES GLACHAN

A CHANCE MEETING

THE last thing Colin Allardyce needed was to be stuck in a carriage full of young kids. Their youthful exuberance meant the atmosphere was crackling as they all enthused about the concert they had been too. Some teeny bopper's heart throb no doubt, he thought as the majority seemed to be girls. If he was told the act's name he probably wouldn't have heard of them.

He had deliberately picked the outside seat of a double seat, hoping to discourage anybody from sitting next to him. Last thing he needed was some spotty oik, stinking of Lynx and pissed with buckfast sitting next to him.

'Excuse me pal, are you keeping that seat for somebody?'

Colin looked up and saw a guy about the same age as him, maybe a bit older.

'No, mate. Hold on, I'll shufty over.'

They sat together and both blew in exasperation at almost the same moment.

'Oh, to be young again,' the late arrival said.

'Long time since we were their age, eh. Whole life ahead of them.'

'Tell you what, they didn't look like that in our day.'

The girls looked to be mostly jailbait, around 16, but how do you tell? All dressed and made-up to look older and most looking as if they were in a competition to show off as much nubile flesh as they could.

Everybody jerked a bit as the train finally pulled away from the Glasgow Central station.

'Oh, I am Terry Carpenter by the way,' the new arrival said, as he stuck out a hand.

'Colin Allardyce,' the other guy proffered.

Although they were squeezed together, Colin offered a fist pump instead of a handshake. Terry held his fist in his hand awkwardly. The worst of Covid might be away, leaving different customs in its wake.

'Shouldn't be so bad after Paisley,' Terry said. 'I spoke to the conductor. One of the other trains was cancelled, that's why there are so many on this one.'

'They are getting off at Paisley. Wish I had done all those years ago. Wouldn't have needed to marry the bitch.'

Getting off at Paisley was the slang for coitus interruptis, the withdrawal method or putting it plainly, pulling out before ejaculation.

Terry let that hang before continuing.

'Got a kid then?'

'Oh, we had a son. Not any longer.'

'Oh, I'm sorry for your loss.'

'No, he didn't die. Would probably have been better if he had. He left home for London as soon as he could.'

There was another awkward silence before Colin continued. 'He's gay.'

Terry didn't know what to say to that.

'I wasn't bothered but Sadie wanted grandchildren and despised him for being gay. You might think that is a bit strong, but she really did despise him. As I said, I wasn't bothered, each to their own has always been my mantra. It was his decision; I will admit I wasn't happy but for his sake I was happy to go along with it.

However, for the sake of our marriage I had to go along with the wife's wishes and that was to literally disown him. Haven't seen or heard from him for more than ten years.'

Terry shook his head, no way would he ever have treated any offspring of his like that.

There was another silence which seemed strange as everyone else in the carriage seemed to be chattering away, still reliving the best bits of the concert they had been to.

'Have you got any kids?'

'No. Not for the want of trying,' Terry said, trying to lighten the mood, and failing.

'We both had tests and they didn't find anything wrong, health wise but, as I said, it just didn't really happen. We even thought about going down the adoption route at one stage but that never happened either.

Angie wanted a baby or a young kid but all they could offer was a teenager.'

Colin looked down the carriage.

'No, you don't want to take on one of those.'

There were a few youngsters standing in the passage as all the seats were filled. Nearest them was a young girl, obviously a teenager, but dressed provocatively and very little being left to the imagination.

'What age do you reckon the blond girl nearest is?' Terry whispered, again trying to change the mood. After all, he was stuck in the train for the next forty minutes or so and needed to lighten the mood for at least a bit of the journey.

'I would reckon she is about 16 or 17. Why?'

'Well, looking at her I realise I am a pervert; I am just trying to gauge how big a pervert I am.'

To Terry's relief Colin laughed along with him.

'Well, at least it doesn't look like I am a pedo,' Terry added.

'Christ man, a young thing like that would kill you or I.'

'Yeah, but what a way to go, eh?'

They both laughed again.

Just at that, as if on cue, the girl turned and although she looked older from behind, facing them she was clearly only about 14. She blew a bubble gum bubble, showing exactly how young she really was.

Just then they felt the train start to slow as they approached Paisley Gilmour Street. As it stopped most of the youngsters quickly streamed off, taking their chattering noise with them, leaving a vacuumess silence behind them.

'What is it you do?' Terry asked as the train started off again.

'I work in sales for a large industrial mob. Normally I am out on the road but once a month we are all in the office for meetings and presentations. We end up in the pub afterwards. What about yourself?'

'Pensions consultant. And yes, at times it is as boring as it sounds. Although part of the job is meeting folk and helping them. Best part is telling them they can retire comfortably earlier than they ever thought they could. Have you got a good pension scheme?'

'Are you trying to sell me some?'

'No, no. It's just surprising how many people didn't save anything until the Government changed the rules a few years ago and forced companies to offer pensions.'

'Well, I must be one of the lucky ones, I have been paying into different schemes since I started work, and that wasn't yesterday.'

'Yes, I know the feeling. Are your pensions all in the one pot?'

Colin shook his head.

'It's something you should really think about. I consolidated all my pensions into one pot. That's the way to go. So, what's the best bit about your job?'

'Well, for one thing I spend a lot of time away from my wife. We are at the stage in our lives when all we seem to do is argue with each other. The more I am away from her the better.'

Colin smirked before continuing. 'Spending a lot of time on the road also means the wife doesn't know where I am all the time. Handy, because I have a lover, well a girlfriend.'

'Serious?'

'Yeah. Mandy and I would be together if Sadie was dead.'

Terry was surprised at the bluntness of the statement. After no doubt many years of marriage like himself, how could he just matter of factly wish his wife dead? Terry could never think like that.

'Why not just split up?'

'Because the cow would be due half of my money. House, savings, pension, the lot. I have worked all my life, since I was sixteen, and she stopped when she got pregnant with our son just after we got married. Never worked since but according to the bastarding law she deserves half. No way is she getting that. Over my dead body. Or hopefully hers.'

Terry was taken aback by the vociferousness in his voice. He must really hate her with a vengeance.

Although the two travellers had obviously been drinking, Terry was surprised about how open Colin had been with his thoughts. Especially to a complete stranger.

'Is your marriage okay?'

'Yes. I am planning to retire within the next year and hoping to move to live in Portugal.'

'Hoping? Why only hoping?'

'Angie, the wife, refuses to even think about moving away while her mother is alive. We holiday in Portugal every year and every time it's harder to return here to Scotland. To the cold weather and constant rain. I am sick of it. You can't beat waking up knowing it's going to be sunny day practically every day, even in the winter, like it is out there.'

'What age is her mother?'

Terry had to think. 'She is either 82 or 83. Apart from being deaf, and getting slower, she seems to be as fit as a fiddle. So, although it's the wrong thing to do, every night I go to bed I hope she dies during the night.'

He felt like adding it was terrible thing to think, but his fellow passenger's attitude was worse, he wanted his wife dead.

'She can't have long to go. However, you could hasten the process.'

'What do you mean?'

Colin looked around to make sure they weren't being overheard.

'Help her on her way.'

'What are you saying, I should kill her?'

'Oh no. Not you.'

'What do you mean then, pay somebody like? No, I couldn't do that.'

'If retiring to Portugal means that much to you it would be worth it.'

Terry shook his head. Anyway, it was 2022, if you so much as fart nowadays they could trace you through your DNA. How could you get away with murder in this day and age?

'Tickets please!'

The conductor's visit interrupted the conversation.

After they showed their tickets there was a long silence between the two. The train rattled on and stopped next at Johnstone.

'Where is it you live?' Terry asked, wondering how long he would need to sit next to this weird guy. Get your mother-in-law murdered, for God's sake. Why would you talk like that to a complete stranger?

'Kilwinning. Do you know Kilwinning?'

'Only to drive through. My wife was from Kilwinning, her mother still lives there.'

'If you know Kilwinning a bit, as you drive out towards Dalry, there are the new houses.'

Terry nodded. New housing estates seemed to be popping up everywhere, this was one of the latest. A sprawling mass of identical kit built identical crap.

'Then there are the older new houses across from them. Well, I live in the even older ones just before them.'

Terry tried to work it out in his head. The load of drink he had swallowed didn't help but he worked out the estate he meant; he had made a few house calls there a few years back, helping people with their pension pots.

'Underwood Road, round that way is it?'

'Yes, that's it. Didn't think you would know it.'

'Yes, I know exactly where you mean. Harry Webb, do you know him? I sorted his pension out a couple of years ago and had to do a house call there.'

Colin shook his head gravely. 'Died last year. Covid.'

'Oh no, he didn't get long after he retired then.'

There was another awkward silence before Colin spoke again.

'What about you, where do you live?'

'I live in Troon.'

'Oh, Troon. Money, money,' he said, rubbing his fingers together, indicating Terry must be minted.

'No, I actually live in an ex-local. I have bought it, of course but it looks good on the business cards though, the Troon address.'

'There is another way.'

'What?'

'Another way to get rid of your mother-in-law. You could swap murders with somebody.'

Terry couldn't believe this guy. He thought they had moved on from the subject. He wasn't going to entertain him anymore, he turned and looked away, hoping he would pick up on the signal.

It didn't work, he continued on the subject.

'Imagine if a complete stranger turned up at your wife's mother's and she passed away, you would be free to fly off to Portugal. Retire sooner and head off to the sun. No more rain, frost, snow.'

There was no danger of them being overheard, the only other passengers left in the compartment apart from them were a young couple sat on the front seats. They had been talking and hugging but now progressed to kissing and God knows what else they were doing as they slid down the seat, out of sight of them.

'Do you think they are married?' Terry asked, pointing to the front of the carriage, again trying to move the conversation away from murder.

'Can't be, they aren't arguing,' Colin said.

'Too true,' Terry agreed, and they both laughed.

'I would kill her if you would kill my wife.'

Terry laughed gently but realised Colin, who had turned to face him, was deadly serious.

'What?'

'Portugal.'

Suddenly, as they headed into the dark Ayrshire countryside, rain battered noisily off the window next to Colin, as if it was a sign, reminding Terry what he wanted to get away from.

'Christ man, this is May, nearly June. It's more like December,' Colin said, turning to stare out at the darkness, trying to get his point across.

As the train slowed to signal they were getting ready to stop at Kilwinning, Colin got out his diary.

'Right, tell you what. I will be on the 6:07 train next Friday. Think about what we said and if you are interested, I will see you then.'

Terry got up and let Colin out to wait for the train to stop. Colin then offered a fist pump again.

'Laters, mate,' he said before leaving the train.

Terry watched Colin walk down the platform with his brolly up to shelter him from the battering rain. Portugal would be nice this time of the year he thought, much better than this.

As he watched Colin walk up the platform stairs to cross the tracks Terry realised Colin had the attributes that were the antithesis of everything he liked in a man.

For a start there was his dress sense. He was wearing a designer suit, not an off the peg job like him. He wore cologne, not aftershave, wore shirts he could only dream of wearing and he had a girlfriend. A lover, a paramour, no doubt younger than the woman he was married to.

He was the kind of guy who could charm the knickers off any woman he wanted to, a patter merchant. For salesman think conman.

Everything he hated in a man Colin was it, yet Terry was still sitting on the train, thinking about teaming up with the guy.

JUST ANOTHER FRIDAY

Terry caught a later train than he usually did the next Friday, the 6:07. He sat in the back carriage, the one nearest the concourse. He wondered if Colin was waiting up in the front carriage as he had arranged.

He was tired. He hadn't slept the previous night. In fact, he hadn't slept much all week. When he set off for Troon station that morning, the rain was off but halfway there the heaven's opened. When he arrived at work that morning he looked and felt like a drowned rat. It reminded him how much he wanted to move to Portugal and how Colin's crazy idea might work.

After 10 minutes, with the train on its way, he got up and walked through the carriage, heading for Colin. Although he had checked him out on the computer, he still didn't know much about him. Was he serious or some Walter Mitty type of character?

He also Googled 'Strangers on a train'. There was a book and a film of the same name, and it turned out one was a psychopath. Maybe that was what Colin was, looking for his next victim.

Terry carried on through the train. He was only going to talk to him after all, they hadn't agreed anything yet.

Colin was sitting in the same double seat they had been in a week before. Terry sat down without speaking.

Initially Colin was annoyed at his personal space being invaded, normally he would have left his briefcase on the seat as he usually did but was expecting Terry. He smiled when he saw who it was.

'I thought you weren't coming.'

'What is it they say, I am intrigued with what you suggested.'

The carriage was busy and there were people on almost every seat. They couldn't talk so openly as they had previously, although most folk had ear plugs in as they checked phones or iPads.

'It's quite simple what I am proposing. I scratch your back.' As he said it he made a gesture with a hand to his throat, as if he was chocking somebody, then added, 'then you scratch mine.'

'Just like that? What if I go first and scratch yours, then you don't scratch mine?'

'Well, I will go first, then you will know I am serious.'

Terry felt his heart thump in his chest as he realised what he could be about to be getting into. He hadn't been so nervous about anything in years.

'Sun, sea and sand awaits, Terry.'

'But I don't know how easy it would be to scratch your back. My back is older than yours, easier to get a result.'

'Although I don't know you too well, I think I know you well enough to do the right thing.'

'Okay, I'm in,' Terry said, then stuck a hand out.

Due to Covid shaking hands had generally been a no-no but this was something that needed agreed with a firm handshake.

Colin smiled although Terry maintained a stern demeanour, aware of the seriousness of the decision they had just agreed on.

'Where does your son live?' Colin asked.

He knew fine well Terry had no kids. After a moment Terry realised this was part of the code they were using.

'He lives alone in a bungalow in Kilwinning. On the Irvine Road.'

'No carers?'

'No, he is capable of looking after himself.'

Colin got his mobile phone out. He put messaging on and pretended to write to his wife.

CCTV in area?, he typed on his phone.

Terry shook his head.

Colin scrubbed that then wrote, Visitors.

'Not at night,' Terry whispered.

Give me her address, he finally wrote.

Terry opened his briefcase and wrote the address on a piece of blank paper then folded it and handed it to him.

'When do you start your new job?' Terry asked. Code for when will you do the business.

Colin shrugged. 'Maybe best you don't know. Then it will be a surprise to you too.'

'Yes, maybe you are right.'

Colin then got his briefcase up from the floor and handed Terry a package from it.

'What's this?' he asked as he looked in the carrier bag.

'Mobile phone. It's pay as you go and there is £20 credit on it. Just for emergencies.'

Terry looked at the phone box and couldn't believe the guy's audacity. How could he have been so sure he would have agreed to this incredulous death pact?

'You are a cocky bastard. How did you know I would agree?'

'Terry, I have been a salesman all my life. First thing you assess is your customer before you work out his or her needs. Although you didn't know it, I saw all the signs you were going to buy into this. I didn't really have to sell you this, deep down you were desperate to buy in.'

Terry looked at the box again and shook his head, before offering the phone back.

'No. You don't know me. I have gone over this in my head time after time. Wondering if I could live with myself and my wife after being complicit in her mother's.'

Terry checked nobody was listening in before adding, 'passing.'

'I get a feeling this is some kind of set up.'

Terry turned to get up and go back to what was now the rear of the train, as far away from Colin as he could get.

Colin tugged him back.

'Tell you what, take the phone. If you don't want to go ahead with our agreement then you have a wee present from me.'

Terry took the phone and walked away back through the train with all kind of thoughts and doubts going through his head. What if he was a plain clothes policeman, trying to set him up? What if Colin did kill his mother-in-law, could he kill somebody in return? Colin's wife, Sadie, what if she was a nice woman? He only had Colin's word for it that she was some kind of ogre who deserved to die.

Strangely, the thought of his mother dying and him heading off into the sunset didn't even come into his mind.

The seat he sat in earlier at the opposite end of the train was still empty. He sat in it for a minute then got up and headed back down the train again.

He plonked himself back next to Colin.

'How do I know who you are?'

Colin took out his wallet and produced his driving licence photo i.d., then rummaged through the papers in his briefcase until he found some headed paper with his name on it.

'Satisfied.'

'Yes, I suppose so.'

The train stopped at Johnstone and the couple sitting in front of Terry and Colin got up and went out.

'Look, take your time. I don't want to rush you, but you have been thinking about it all week and you came to me. I always think things happen for a reason and we were put together last week. Don't for a minute think I am forcing your arm, I am not. The decision is yours.'

'Yes I know. Right, I am in.'

NIGHT-NIGHT INA

Colin had driven past Ina's house 3 times before parking up 2 streets away. From the boot of the car, he took out his hi-viz jacket and hard hat. Normally they were reserved for site visits he did for work but tonight he was going to use it to gain entry to his target's house. He decided on the ploy of being hidden in plain sight.

Colin walked confidently through the streets although he crossed over when anybody approached. He didn't want any witnesses who could put him in the area that night.

As he got closer to her house he felt the adrenalin start to course through his veins. It might be an old woman, but he was going to kill her. Squeeze the life out of her decrepit old body. He was actually getting sexually aroused by the thought.

From outside the house, he could see the living room lit up and the television on with the sound turned up really loud. Obviously the old dear was a bit mutton jeff.

As he got closer to the house it was clear that the volume was at its maximum level, she must be stone deaf. He was worried it might be hard to get her attention without drawing attention to himself, the last thing he wanted.

He knocked on the door a couple of times before tapping gently on the window.

He could see through the hall window the living room door open and the old woman shuffle through.

When she finally unlocked the door and opened it Colin held up a false identity card he had made up.

'Good evening madam. I'm from Scottish Water. Your neighbours reported their cold water was dirty. Is yours okay?'

'What?'

Colin sighed deeply then looked around, hoping he hadn't drawn attention to himself.

He tried again. 'I am from Scottish Water!,' he said, pointing to his fake i.d and speaking louder than he wanted to.

'What's wrong?'

Hoping she wouldn't be alarmed he moved forward, inviting himself in.

Naturally Ina stepped back, giving him space to enter.

He leaned in close.

'I am from Scottish Water. Your neighbour said their water was dirty. Is yours okay?'

'Oh, right son. The water.'

Ina said, nodding that she understood and turned and went into the bathroom that was behind them, opposite the front door.

Colin pushed the front door closed with his elbow and pulled a pair of blue disposable gloves from his jacket pocket and stepped up behind Ina.

The old woman had the cold water running and saw it was clear. Before she could turn her head, Colin's left arm snaked round and clamped her neck. His right-hand went over her mouth and thumb and first finger pinched her nose, stopping her breathing.

Beneath his grip, he felt the life slip out of the old woman's body. Looking in the mirror in front of him he saw he was smiling as he held his limp, lifeless trophy in his arms. He couldn't believe how easy it had been.

Initially, he planned to just leave the body where she died but he suddenly had a great idea. Put her in bed, as if she died naturally in her sleep.

The body was light but even Colin had to drag her through to her bed. He popped off her dressing gown and slippers and put her in her bed.

Just as he pulled the bed covers back over, the phone on the dressing room table buzzed into life.

Colin's heart skipped a beat. He stood transfixed, as if suddenly captured. He held his breath as the phone buzzed another twice then went silent.

When he regained his composure he went round and put the television and lights off before slipping out into the night. Job done.

I'M WORRIED ABOUT MUM

Terry was watching Still Game on the BBC Scotland iplayer. He had seen all the episodes more than once but there was sod all else on worth watching.

Angie, who had gone up to bed half an hour earlier, appeared back down at the living room door.

'I'm worried about mum.'

'What?'

He hit mute on the remote.

'She hasn't phoned me back.'

'What are you talking about?'

'I ring her, let it ring three times, then she rings me back, lets it ring three times then she hangs up.'

'Maybe she is sleeping.'

'She wouldn't go to sleep without ringing me, that's our system. I have phoned her five times and it's just ringing out. We need to go over there.'

'How long have you been doing this?'

'What, the phone thing? Since last year. I told you. Don't say I didn't. You know your problem, you don't listen.'

'What about her neighbour? Mrs. Gibson, has she not got a key?'

'It's Mrs. Gilbert, and she went in a home last year. That was why I started phoning her. She's got a new neighbour now. God, you are terrible.'

'Well, I suppose we better get over there.'

'Sorry if I am bothering you,' Angie said, before storming out to get dressed again.

Terry got his jacket and shoes on and went out and got the car out of the drive.

Angie got in the car and slammed the door shut.

Terry reached out and tapped her knee. 'Ang, she will be okay. Your mother is as tough as old boots.'

Angie said nothing but dabbed at her eyes.

As Terry sat in his car, waiting as his wife locked the front door, he got a sinking feeling in his stomach. She was dead. When Angie came downstairs it hadn't dawned on him when she said about her mother not answering the phone he didn't think Colin would have done it so quick, not the next Tuesday.

Terry felt sick, Colin had carried out his half of the bargain.

Now that the desire had become the reality it suddenly dawned on him what he had to deal with. Angie would be absolutely distraught.

When she got in he drove off mechanically, other things on his mind.

'Terry!' Angie screamed.

Terry hit the brakes.

'It's red!'

Just then a taxi shot past him, he was seconds from a collision. He looked at the traffic light. She was right, he had been about to drive through a red light.

'Oh my God. What's going on with you?'

'I'm just worried about your mum.'

'No, you are not, you were dreaming. Take me back home. I am going to get a taxi.'

The lights turned to green, and Terry drove on, ignoring her. Still shaken, but now he was concentrating fully on his driving.

'What if there is something wrong with your mum? Is the taxi driver going to help you?'

'Well, watch the road then!'

Once on the bypass, Terry wanted to floor it, but Angie was sitting with her arms folded, waiting for him to make another mistake so she could have another go at him.

It would be just his luck to get caught speeding, so he kept within the speed limit, not chancing it.

Kilwinning was less than ten miles from their Troon home, they would be there in no time anyway.

As they neared the Kilwinning turn off, Terry pulled over and shot past the slip road.

'You've missed the turn off!' Angie shouted.

'No, Ang, it's quicker to go down the bypass, round the roundabout and go back down the Industrial Estate way,' Terry said in a calming voice.

'I suppose,' Angie muttered, almost apologetically.

Outside her mother's house they parked the car. Terry wanted to go in first but as soon as the car stopped Angie was out the car and running towards the house with the door key in her hand.

The house was in darkness. Terry vowed if she was alive he was going to call the whole thing off. Going to Portugal wasn't worth this.

'Please be alive,' he whispered to himself as he reached the front door.

The blood-curdling scream from inside told him his request was in vain. He found his wife kneeling by the bed, running a hand down her mother's now cold cheek.

'Oh, mum,' she sobbed, 'oh no, mum.'

Terry burst into tears and kneeled beside her, putting an arm round his wife's shoulder.

After 5 minutes Terry got up, leaving his wife who was now running a hand through her mother's fine, white hair. A few minutes later she got up and they cuddled, and both cried again.

'At least she is at peace,' Terry said. He knew it sounded crass, but he couldn't think of anything else to say.

'What do we do now? Phone 999?'

'I suppose so. I don't know, I have never found anybody dead before. I will do it through the room.'

Terry walked through to the kitchen; he didn't want distress Angie anymore. When he got his phone out he realised his hand was shaking. He had to try 3 times to unlock his phone. His hand was shaking so much he was hitting the wrong numbers on the log-in screen.

'Accident and emergency, which service do you require?'

'Eh, I don't know. We just found my mother-in-law dead in her bed.'

'You are sure there is no sign of life?'

'No, she is cold.'

'Right sir. I need your mothers-in-law's details.'

Terry told the woman everything she needed.

'Okay sir, we will get the police there with you as soon as possible.'

'The police?'

'It's nothing to worry about sir, it's just the procedure.'

Terry hung up then had a thought. Maybe she had just died in her sleep. She looked as if she had. But Angie's phone call. If she phoned the previous night, she could have died the night before, after she phoned her. Maybe Colin hadn't killed her. There was no sign of foul play.

Angie was still in her mother's bedroom. She had stopped crying and was just staring at her mother.

'The police are on their way.'

'Something's not right.'

'What?'

'She has still got her teeth in.'

There was a glass of water on the bedside table next to the phone.

'Maybe she was too tired and forgot to take them out.'

Angie looked at him. Her incredulous expression told him he was in trouble again.

'You really don't know my mother. She might not have ever had much to speak of, but she had dignity and she was so particular about her appearance. She would never have gone to bed with her teeth in. She wouldn't have, it's just not right.'

''What are you saying?' Terry asked. The last thing Terry wanted was his wife stirring things up.

'I don't know what I am saying!' she said, losing her temper with him again.

They were disturbed by a knock on the front door.

KNOCK KNOCK

Terry opened the front door to find two young policewomen. He had never believed the saying about police officers getting younger until that moment.

The younger looked as if she had left school, the older girl was probably just in her twenties, and both looked glammed up for a night out.

'Mister Rankin.'

'No, I am Terry Carpenter. Mrs. Rankin is, was, my mother-in-law.'

'Right. Very sorry.'

He stood back and let them in. As they walked past the waft of their perfumes was overpowering.

'She is through there,' he said, pointing to the now closed bedroom door.

The older cop went through while the other went through to the living room, to speak to his wife.

Terry stood in the hall, waiting for the policewoman's hypothesis, hoping she was convinced it was natural causes. She spoke on her mobile but even with the door now ajar he still couldn't make out what she was saying.

When she walked through Terry realised she wasn't as young as he first thought. She was very attractive and under different circumstances she would be fanciable, but right then things were too serious for any trivia like that.

She walked through to the living room and Terry followed.

'Mister and Mrs. Carpenter, I assume you weren't here when your mother died?'

She was looking at Angie, who shook her head gently.

'As this is a sudden death I would ask you if you could go back to your car for a few minutes while we check things out.'

'Why?' Terry asked, suddenly suspicious.

'Just procedure, sir. We need to check there hasn't been a break-in. We should only be a few minutes.'

Terry walked slowly behind his wife, and they headed out to sit in his car.

'Told you there was something dodgy,' Angie said.

Terry said nothing. He thought it was just procedural, after all they had to check the house, but there was no point in arguing with Angie while she was in her current state.

They watched the cops moving about in the house before going out the front and checking the door and windows, before waving them to come back over.

'There is no sign of a break-in, our next step is to call in and ask for the local doctor to come out and sign the death certificate.'

'What, are they not sending paramedics or an ambulance?' Angie said anxiously.

'No. Things have changed because of Covid. We are all trained in advanced first aid. We do the initial assessment and as she is dead there is no point in wasting the medical resources. As I said the doctor will sign the death certificate then you will need to phone the undertaker and arrange for the undertaker to get the body uplifted.'

Angie stormed away from the group, annoyed she wasn't being listened to. The elder copper nodded to the other girl to go and speak to her.

'Thanks. This is all new to us,' Terry said.

'Of course, sir. You don't think about things like this until they happen. Why would you?'

She then signalled to Terry to hang fire, to wait a few minutes before going through to the living room.

When they walked through they found Angie in a better mood, sitting on the settee with the young copper.

'Terry, do you remember Andy Tonner? This is his youngest, Rita.'

They exchanged smiles.

'Rita said we should phone the Co-op now. Save waiting until the Doctor comes, that could be a couple of hours.'

'Best phone now then. Do you want me to call them?'

'Yes. I found the leaflet, it's on the mantlepiece there.'

Terry went through to the kitchen again for privacy. As he spoke to the man from the Co-op, he could hear raised voices from the living room. No doubt Angie getting angry as she insisted her mother was a victim of foul play.

When Terry started his car's engine it was after 4 o'clock and the new day was starting to dawn. Light drizzle started and he hit the wipers.

'I still can't believe it,' Angie said as she plonked herself in the passenger seat.

'I know, it was so sudden.'

'No, not that, well, that is a shock but those two policewomen, well policekids, wouldn't listen to me when I said there was something iffy about mum's death. Then the doctor agreed with them. He just wanted back to his bed, didn't want to listen either. That was bad enough but then he wrote cause of death was Covid because she tested positive a fortnight ago. What a crock of shit.'

Terry knew better than to disagree with her.

'I know. They cover each other's backs.'

'Oh, speak up now. I didn't hear you sticking up for me in there!'

'Well, they said if you wanted to pursue it they would need to do a post-mortem. Surely you don't want your mother's body cut up?'

'No, but they just didn't listen to me. You didn't back me up either.'

Terry drove off but what she said was niggling him.

'You know something, if I speak up it's wrong and if I don't it's a fault too. I just can't win with you.'

'It's not about winning; it's about supporting me.'

For the rest of the journey the silence was deafening, the atmosphere frostier than a snowman's nose.

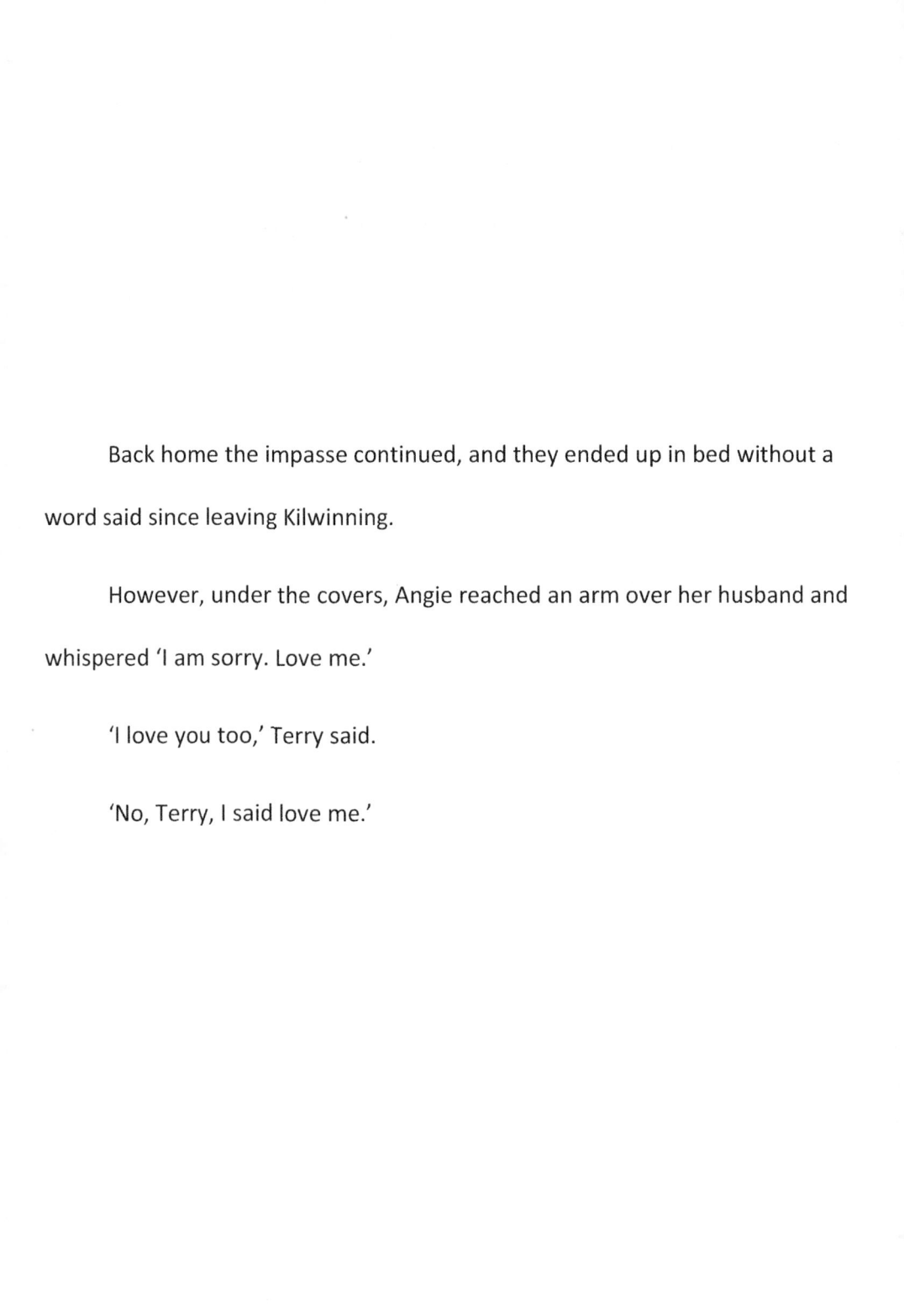

Back home the impasse continued, and they ended up in bed without a word said since leaving Kilwinning.

However, under the covers, Angie reached an arm over her husband and whispered 'I am sorry. Love me.'

'I love you too,' Terry said.

'No, Terry, I said love me.'

MY MUM WAS MURDERED

Monday morning and Terry left for work as normal. As he walked to the station, for the first time since he headed to Kilwinning to find his mother-in-law's dead body, he allowed himself a smile.

It had been ropey at times, Angie kept insisting her mother was a victim of foul play. Despite what the police officers and the doctor said on the Wednesday night to assured her it was natural causes and old age that brought about her death, she was still adamant they were wrong. It was only when they said she would need a post-mortem that she went along with them. The thought of her mother being cut up was too much for her to bear.

The early morning sun, though, wasn't enough to keep him happy. Although it was late May, there was still a biting wind that was hastening him toward the sanctuary of the station but, longer term, to sunny Portugal.

He just needed to bide his time with Angie and let her grieve for her mother before broaching the subject.

What also bore heavy on his mind was the fact he now had to reciprocate and kill Sadie Allardyce.

As soon as Terry was out of sight Angie phoned her cousin, Karen. Her cousin spoke first after seeing Angie's name flash up on her phone screen.

'Hi love. I heard about your mother. I am so sorry; she was a wee gem of a woman.'

'Thanks. She was love, like your mother, she was a gem of a woman too. Listen, the reason I am phoning is, well, your John is still in the police, isn't he?'

'Yes. He retires next year. I am not looking forward to having him under my feet all the time, I can tell you. Why?'

'Well, between you and me I don't think my mum died naturally.'

'Really?'

'The thing is nobody wants to believe me. My mother and I did the three rings every night so we both knew she was okay. You know what I mean?'

'Yes, I do it with our Stacey if she is out for the night.'

'Well, the night she died she didn't. When we went round to hers she was in bed with her teeth still in.'

'Is that it?'

'Oh, I thought you would have understood, what with your old mother dying last year from Covid. You were never away from hers. You knew your mother's wee foibles and I know there is no way mum would have gone to bed with her teeth in. Especially when she had a glass sitting on the bedside cabinet with fresh steradent in it.'

'Did they take anything?'

'No. That's why nobody believes me! I have been on the internet; folk do things like this for kicks. Or they just want to get away with murder, you know, commit the perfect murder, the one nobody solves.'

'Mind you, your mother was like mine. They never had much but they always turned out immaculate. Right, tell you what, I will speak to John, get him to have a wee look into it.'

'Thanks love.'

DEAD END JOB

Detective Sergeant John Rose sat at his desk in his office, looking over old crime cases. Calling it an office though was a stretch, he was in a converted storage cupboard upstairs in the Saltcoats police station. It didn't even have a window.

He had been lumbered there for two months as he was slowing down, as the bosses called it, as he headed towards his retirement.

Nobody would say it, but the real reason was he had stuck his head above the parapet and complained the detectives were understaffed and overworked. The bosses didn't want to hear that, this was the reward.

His mobile vibrated in his pocket. Karen. No doubt wanting something from the shops on his way home.

'Hi love. Remember I told you last week about our Angie's mother dying.'

Something in the back of his mind registered. He couldn't remember who this Angie or her mother were but did remember she said something along the lines of that's another funeral we need to go to.

'Why?'

'Well, Angie just phoned me. She thinks there was some kind of foul play. Says her mother was murdered.'

John's mood suddenly perked up. Whether it was a genuine case or not he was making it one. A chance to get out of the office and talk to folk and actually get to do some real police work.

'Right, love, give me the details you have.'

Karen reeled off Angie and her mother's details before adding she wanted him to get her a brown loaf from the shops on the way home.

John hated going to the shops but now had a case to work on, that made up for it.

First thing he checked the log from the previous Tuesday night. The two officers that attended were P.C.'s H. Begg and R. Tonner. Offhand, John didn't know them. Over the past few years, the police college seemed to be churning out new recruits, quicker than he could keep up with them.

He went down to the communal office and asked the duty sergeant when they were next on duty. As luck would have it, Helen Begg was in the office at that time. Her mate was off for the next two days. Speaking to one of them would be enough, John thought.

He walked over. Before he could introduce himself and explain what he wanted he overheard Helen talking excitedly about the previous night's Love Island episode. John despaired, officers like her were exactly the reason he would be glad to get out.

'Sorry to bother you Helen. I am Detective Sergeant John Rose. I am looking into the death of Ina Ralston.'

Helen stared at him blankly. Obviously this Ina wasn't a contestant, if that was their designation, on Love Island, so she would need prompting.

'Last Tuesday night in Kilwinning.'

'Right. The old lady who was found in bed.'

Suddenly she thought she was being investigated by the D.S., as if she had been done something wrong.

'Why, has there been a complaint?'

'No, no, nothing like that. Were there any signs of a struggle, anything unusual?'

The other copper got her notebook and flicked through the pages before reading from her notes.

'Attended at approx. 22:30. Lady was lying in bed, wearing nightclothes. No sign of break in or any foul play.'

John stifled a laugh, foul play, what were they teaching these young coppers at the college, he thought.

'Her daughter insisted she had been killed because she had her teeth in and hadn't phoned her before going to bed.'

'There were no signs of anything else suspicious?'

'No. The daughter, though, was quite insistent something was wrong, but my colleague explained if she wanted to continue following this line her mother would need a post-mortem examination.

The duty G.P. appeared at 00:05 and declared she had died of natural causes and proceeded to give them the death certificate. We sent our report to the procurator fiscal and that was the end of it.'

'Fine, thanks very much, P.C Begg.'

John walked back to his office. Anybody else would have left it at that but something piqued his interest. He got his jacket, made sure he had his keys and left for Ina's house.

On the train, Terry switched on the phone Colin had given him. It beeped immediately. Colin had sent him a text on the Thursday morning. It simply said, YOUR TURN NEXT.

Terry replied. They hadn't agreed on the type of code they would use, so simply said: Complications, you shouldn't have put baby to bed. Enquiries ongoing.

He smiled to himself as he hit the send button. Angie had been convinced there was something unusual about her mother's death. He had kept quiet, kind of agreeing with her but definitely not arguing that she was wrong.

It was only when she thought that to continue with her protestation would mean her mother's body being cut up that she went with what the doctor and two female cops had said.

John parked his car round the corner from Ina's house. The bungalow was the middle one in a row of five. He walked up the path in front of the houses. He had never been in one of those one-bedroom bungalows so didn't know the layout. Hopefully one of the neighbours would help.

He knocked on the neighbours to the left-hand side. The door opened almost immediately, obviously one of the unofficial neighbourhood watch members.

The old dear was at least 70, white hair in a net and a worried look on her face.

John showed her his i.d. card.

'Sorry to bother you madam, I am sure you know your neighbour was found dead last Wednesday night.'

'Yes. I heard about it the next morning. I only moved in here 6 months ago and didn't really know her mother, but she seemed a nice lady.'

'Oh yes, apparently she was. Now, did you notice anything unusual on Tuesday night?'

The old lady looked down at her slippers before answering.

'I heard voices about 9 o'clock. You see she was deaf. Her television was always so loud I knew what programme she was watching. Just after 9 there was voices.'

'Voices?'

'I was going to bed and was just shutting the living room curtains but I looked out but couldn't see who was there. One of the voices was hers. Because she is deaf she talks very loudly. Then about 10 minutes after that the television went off and all was quiet. That was early for her, she usually stayed up until about 10 o'clock.'

'Right.'

'Sorry, I can't help you any more than that.'

'No, maybe you have helped. Thanks.'

John turned and walked away, thinking as he went.

Terry unlocked the phone when the new message beeped.

YOU CANT RENAGE, A DEAL IS A DEAL !!!!

Terry turned his phone closer to his body. Although nobody was near him he wanted what he typed to be kept secret.

He replied simply, Be patient. Then he switched the phone off.

John went to the one of the other neighbours, on the right-hand side. His face lit up as he walked down the path. They had a Ring doorbell. If it recorded as well as alerting he might get something, although he still didn't know what.

The nameplate on the door said R.Murphy. John hoped he wasn't Irish, often he struggled to understand their accents because they spoke too quickly.

The man of the house opened the door before John had even knocked it.

He was a jovial looking man, dressed in a string vest with suit trousers and bright yellow braces.

His smile dropped when John showed his police identity photocard.

'Good morning sir. Sorry to bother you but I am looking into the death of Mrs. Ralston.'

'Oh, is it suspicious?' he asked in a strong Scottish brogue, much to John's relief.

'No, we just need to follow up every sudden death.'

John didn't believe in lying to anyone when he was on duty. He consoled himself by thinking he wasn't lying, just bending the truth a bit.

'Did you see or hear anything last Tuesday night?'

'No. We were away at my daughter's caravan until Friday.'

'What about your doorbell? Did you get any alerts?'

'The thing is, if anybody so much as walks the nearest side of the pavement it alerts. I just give it a quick check. Unless they are walking up our path I don't bother with it.'

'Does it record?'

As soon as he said it, this old guy was the last person he expected to be computer savvy and expected a laugh and a no, or a don't know.

'Oh yes. I back everything up.'

Very promising, the cop thought.

'Could we have a look?'

'Sure, come in.'

The living room was small but fitted in a small table and chairs at one end, a settee in the middle and a large computer table at the front window.

'Take a seat. I will need to get this thing started.'

'Russell, are you at that bloody computer again!' his wife called through. She stopped when she popped her head through and saw they had a visitor. 'Oh, sorry.'

'This is Detective Sergeant John Rose. He wants to see if we got anything recorded on the doorbell.'

John was surprised he had picked that up from having a quick look at his i.d. card. Mind must be sharp as a pin.

'What's wrong?'

'There's something iffy about Ina's death.'

'Really?'

John felt a bit like a tennis umpire as the two old folk batted their comments between themselves, as if he wasn't there. Although suddenly he had the wifie's full attention.

'Just checking a few things,' he said before being asked, as it still wasn't officially "iffy."

'Would you like a coffee?'

John shook his head while her hubby was quick to say yes.

'I wasn't asking you,' she said before joining John sitting on the setee.

'What's this?' the old guy said.

On the screen was a workman, hi-viz jacket and hard hat, on the pavement, heading towards Ina's house. John joined the old man and stood looking over his shoulder.

'What time was that?'

'Just after 9 o'clock.'

'Can you scroll forward, see if we catch him going the other way.'

Surely enough, about 15 minutes later he is captured walking the opposite way. This time he was still wearing the hi-viz but was also wearing blue nitrile gloves.

'That's strange, the old guy said, pointing to the gloves on the screen.

'Can you capture those images and email them to me?'

'Never done it but it should be easy,' the old man said confidently.

'Can you check to see if there are anybody else in the next few minutes who might have passed them.'

The next image was a bulldog, 2 minutes later.

'Do you know whose dog that is?'

The old man shook his head.

'Sammy Thompson!' his wife, who had joined them, and was looking over her husband's other shoulder, suddenly piped up.

'Where does he live?'

'At the bottom of the row, in number 2.'

'Right, I need a word with him next. Here is my card, the email address is at the bottom. If you have any issues give me a call and let me know, I can always get one of our experts from the tech department out to help you.'

The old couple accompanied him through to the front door.

'Are you sure you don't want a coffee?' the old dear asked, trying to delay him, keen to maybe eek out some more info that she could use as gossip.

'No, I must get on.'

At the end of the row his arrival was welcomed by the boxer barking madly behind the front door.

The dog was obviously pushed through to the lounge. The barking didn't stop but was diffused a bit.

'Sorry to bother you sir, Detective Sergeant John Rose. I was wondering if you remember seeing a man last Tuesday night.'

The old guy, who looked like an adult version of one of the dwarfs although more grizzled, looked a bit Sleepy but had more a look of Dopey.

John went on. 'Just after 9 o'clock. Maybe you saw a works van or lorry at around that time.'

'Tuesday. I remember now. The guy put his head down when he passed me. He was about your size and build. Don't know how old he was because he had a hard hat and mask thing on.'

'Did you know where he went?'

'I kept a wee eye on him because he looked dodgy. He crossed over and went down Union Street, probably parked next to the shops down there.'

'Thanks for that sir. I might need to come back and get a statement if things develop.'

Grumpy said nothing else and promptly closed the door.

John wasn't bothered about his attitude; he had another lead to follow. An old woman being killed might not bother a lot of folk, but if investigating it was the alternative to sitting in the office pouring over boring, cold case files, he would give it his all.

SURPRISE

Terry held the phone Colin gave him in his hand. He hated it; it was the symbol that reminded him he was in this thing further than he wanted to. Technically, he had arranged his mother-in-law's death, just so he could move to sunnier climes. Unfortunately, now, he had to kill Colin's wife before he could go.

Terry was the kind of guy who wouldn't even squash a spider, Terry who would go out of his way to remove errant arachnids from the house. If he couldn't kill a defenceless creature, how could he ever kill a human being?

With the phone off, there was no way for Colin to contact him. If he did he was establishing a link between them, one that could get them both in trouble. Deep down he knew he couldn't ignore it for ever. To try to ensure he didn't meet Colin he would get a much earlier train. He made an excuse in the office he had toothache and had a late dental appointment.

The earlier train was a lot quieter than the normal commuter ones. Terry had a seat to himself and sat at the window seat, confident that nobody would join him.

The phone. He stared at it again, wondering why he had even thought about agreeing a deal with Colin.

'Switch it on!' was hissed menacingly in his ear.

The phone flipped into the air as it slipped out of his hand at the surprise. Luckily, or maybe unluckily, he caught it again.

Before he looked round he knew it was Colin who sat himself down next to him. Squeezing up, invading his personal space, jamming him next to the window.

'All right. If I knew you liked me that much we could have booked a hotel room in town.'

'Don't get funny with me. I have done my part of the bargain; you need to do yours.'

Terry had thought of a stalling strategy, now was the time to try it.

'There are complications. You made a mess of it?'

'How?'

'I told you, you put her to bed. She still had her false teeth in, she never went to bed with her teeth in.'

'That's it? She couldn't have felt ill and slipped into bed early.'

'That's what I suggested but my wife was having none of it. Said I knew nothing about her mother.'

Colin muttered 'for fucks sake,' under his breath.

'Then there is the three rings thing.'

'I never touched any jewellery. Was something missing?'

'No, on the phone. Angie and her mother would signal each other. They would phone each other at night, give it three rings then hang up. Obviously Isa didn't phone back, that was why we had to rush over to her house the night you, did it.'

'Now you tell me.'

Colin was angry because the phone rang. He could have called back and given three rings that night when he was in her house.

'I didn't know about it. Angie said she told me ages ago, but I don't think she did.'

Colin, for once, never said anything. Members of the husband's union would always agree they were accused of not listening so he couldn't disagree with him on that point.

They travelled in silence for a few minutes before Colin put the squeeze on again, pinning Terry against the side of the carriage for a second time.

'I am going with your story for the moment, but I want to warn you, if you are dicking me around, well I know people.'

He spoke with a menacing, quiet tone that scared Terry for a trice before responding, also in a whisper.

'If you are so clever and you know people as you say, why did you not get them to knock off your wife?'

'Do you think I am stupid? Who would be the prime suspect? Me. If there was any little thing to lead it back to me, I would get the blame. That's a risk I cannot afford to take, that's why you will do it for me.'

'Look, my wife's old mother has just passed. She needs me by her side. Give me a couple of weeks, that's all I ask, then you will get your wish.'

'Right, two weeks today we meet on the 6:07 train again. Then we will get it organised.'

'Sure.'

Colin backed off, moving along the seat, letting Terry breath again.

John Rose walked in with the loaf of brown bread he had been ordered to get.

'What's wrong with you?'

'Nothing. Why?'

'You are smiling. You usually come home from work with a face like a smacked arse.'

'You know, your cousin might be right.'

'Really?'

'Yes. Something doesn't ring true although apart from a picture of a stranger in hi-viz gear I don't have any evidence.'

'Are they letting you look into it then?'

'Well, I haven't asked, but that won't stop me. I am sick and tired of sitting in a cupboard for an office all day, every day.'

'So, what comes next?'

'I am going to speak to your cousin tomorrow morning.'

'Make sure you tell her I am asking for her.'

'Of course.'

A DETECTIVE SERGEANT CALLS

Angie had the front door opened before John had even rung the doorbell.

'Is it good news, John?' Angie asked excitedly, recognising her cousin's husband from previous family events.

John barely remembered the blond standing in the doorway waiting on him. According to Karen they had been at a few social functions, but John was sure he would have remembered Angie.

'Best we talk inside, eh.'

'Sure,' she smiled, then she stepped aside and let him past.

John compared Angie to his wife. They were about the same height, but Angie was a bit heavier. Karen though, was a smoker, they say that supresses an appetite and maybe why she was thinner.

Angie also had nicer skin and juicier boobs and wore classier clothes. Like Karen, Angie had obviously been a stunner in an earlier life but was no way disagreeable now. Her looks might have mellowed with age, but he thought she was still very easy on the eye.

The previous night, cheered by his result of getting the pictures, and having a real case to work, he hoped Karen would come across with his marital needs. Before he could get round to broaching the subject she disappeared up to bed with "one of her heads."

John used to joke it wasn't her head he wanted but that now fell flatter than a lead balloon. It left him, however, sexually frustrated.

John sat on the sofa, which was a large, expensive leather job. He pulled the pictures from the large brown envelop he was carrying.

The old guy had emailed them, and they were top notch quality.

'Do you recognise this guy from any of these two photos?'

Angie sat next to him. John immediately caught a noseful of her perfume. Strangely, he thought, she smelled exactly how he thought she would, subtle but alluring.

Karen hadn't come across with the marital needs for nearly a month and John had reached the desperate stage where he found himself imagining having sex with every woman he met. Angie was certainly no exception.

At these close quarters, with knees almost touching, he felt he was getting aroused. He just hoped it didn't show.

Angie, meantime, was carefully studying the pictures, looking from one to the other.

'No. It's hard to tell with the hat and mask on. Are you sure I should know him?'

John gave a disappointing look.

'This could possibly be your mother's killer.'

'Really? Why is he wearing hi-viz gear, did he work on a building site?'

'Don't know, but we call it being invisible in plain view. He could, of course, have been visiting one of your mother's neighbours but I covered most of them yesterday. However, this guy seems to have been in the vicinity at the time of your mother's death.

Then there's the blue gloves. Why would he be wearing them?'

Angie stared again with renewed interest.

'Right, I see them now. Who could he be then?'

John raised his hands, showing he didn't have an idea. Not the way a policeman should act but this was personal to him now, and he wanted to level with her.

'I am quite sure you would have said, but is there any reason anybody would want your mum dead?'

'No. Everybody loved her?'

'Did she have a carer?'

'No, she was fiercely independent. Would hardly let us do anything for her, certainly she wouldn't have a stranger in her house.'

'Her neighbour caught these images on his Ring doorbell. The guy at the end of the row saw him walk towards the Spar shop over the road. I tried them but there cctv was broken. What I need to do is try and get cctv from somewhere else that maybe shows the guy driving away from the area and get his car registration from that.'

As John was speaking Angie was still looking at the pictures. Although the guy's face was covered she kept looking in case there was something that might trigger some recognition, maybe his body language, the way he seemed to be walking, but she came up blank.

'I would appreciate it that you kept this information to yourself Angie. This is strictly between us, I am going out on a limb on this, I shouldn't be investigating it.'

'Oh no, John. I won't tell a soul. Thanks for doing this.'

'Right, I need to get going, do a bit of my day job. But rest assured I will spend as much time as I can on this. If it turns out to be coincidence then it will just be between us, but I have a feeling there is more to this than meets the eye.'

John suddenly realised he had done the opposite; he had told Karen. He would tell her that night Angie didn't know the guy and they had agreed to finish it.

'Where are my manners, I haven't even offered you a coffee.'

'No thanks, Angie. As I said, I better get going, see what else I can find out.'

The real reason he wanted out was that he was getting too aroused. Everything about his wife's cousin was turning him on. The way she looked, dressed, smelled, smiled. No, he had to get out before he did something he would regret.

Angie got up with him and showed him to the door.

As he walked out he tried to keep facing away from Angie to try and hide the growing bulge in his pants.

'Thanks for doing this John,' she said as they stood at the front doorway.

John looked into her eyes. Pools of blue he would love to dive into.

'You are the only person who has listened to me, and I appreciate it. I really do. If you get to the bottom of this I will be grateful. Very grateful.'

'I will, be, be in touch,' he said, stammering a bit now as he tried not to read into what she said as the very thing he desired.

John walked down the path with a spring in his step. Angie was offering more than a bottle of whisky for his help; he was sure she was offering herself.

He realised he was in lust with her. Although he had already been on board and thought he was onto something, he vowed to himself he would do everything in his power to solve this whodunnit. The reward would definitely be worth the effort.

Halfway back to the office John stopped in a layby and relieved himself, imagining as he did so, getting his reward from Angie.

A LITTLE SECRET

Angie's hand shook a little as she put the key in the lock on her mother's front door. It was only the second time she had been there since she found her mother's body and still dreaded it.

Detective Sergeant John Rose was with her. He phoned later the previous day and arranged to meet her at her mother's house that Thursday morning. He had been waiting outside for her when she got there, she liked his keenness.

It was strange how the house she loved visiting had now become quite suddenly the place she dreaded being in most. She had to get over her dread, the house needed to be emptied soon as the Council would no doubt start hounding her for the keys, even though the rent was fully paid up for a few weeks yet.

While Angie went through to the living room, the policeman checked out the bedroom where the dead woman was found.

He opened the curtains wide and put the light on to get the room as well-lit as possible. Everything was exactly as he would have expected to find on a sudden death.

He closed the curtains and put the room back the way he found it.

In the bathroom he swabbed the taps and inside the sink. If the guy thought he was so clever as to have committed the perfect murder he might have gotten too cocky and made a mistake thinking he could wash away his DNA.

Although the guy might have kept his gloves on, he might have rubbed his face and transferred his DNA onto his gloves then the taps. It might be a long shot but in modern criminal investigation it was now more about gathering evidence than actually investigating crimes.

Angie meantime had been looking through some of her mum's papers, insurance and documents like that, she had found in an old shortbread tin.

She looked up expectantly when John walked in. 'Well?'

John shrugged. 'No sign of a struggle. You said nothing had been taken. However, with what you said about your mother she sounds a bit like mine was. A creature of habit you would say.'

'Has your mother passed?'

'Yes. Eighteen months ago. They blamed Covid but she died in hospital. You come out of there, if you make it, worse than when you went in. She didn't make it out, though.'

'So, what now?'

'Well, I get these samples analysed. Have you got your mother's hairbrush?'

'What for?'

'To eliminate her DNA from any we might find.'

'It will be through in her room.'

'Do you want me to get it?'

Angie nodded. Going back in the house had been hard enough, touching something personal like that would have sent her over the edge. Terry would need to help her clear the house; it was all too personal for her.

'It will be in the top drawer of the bedside cabinet,' she called through after him.

As John returned he slipped the evidence bag into his pocket, trying not to alarm Angie any more than she appeared to be.

She held a piece of paper to him.

'What do you make of that?'

It was an official looking document and he quickly scanned it, a skill he always had.

'To me it looks like she has signed over 10 per cent of what little she has to this local cancer charity. Was that a charity she favoured?'

'No. She was always giving to children's or heart charities. Dad died of a heart attack, and she liked to support them but never cancer support. She never mentioned this to me. Do you think this is some kind of scam? Getting old and vulnerable people to sign up to this?'

'I have never heard of it, but I will pass the details on to the community support officer. I think it's a woman for this area.'

'I mean what do they think she has? Look round about you? Has she hidden thousands in the bank, gold bullion under her bed? You know to think, after 83 years on this earth and all she has to show for it is a few quid she had in her purse, a few hundred in the bank and an insurance policy that will probably just pay to bury her and get her headstone.'

Angie started welling up then dropped her head as the tears started to flow.

John moved over and took her in her arms.

This was the release she needed, and her body convulsed as she broke down.

John held her and patted her back gently while whispering, 'I know, I know, she is gone.'

After several minutes she stopped crying. She turned her head up, looked into John's eyes and simply said, 'thanks.'

She leaned her head forward and, without saying anything, kissed him on the lips. He kissed back.

Their osculations interrupted abruptly by a ringing in the house as the noise of the doorbell rang loudly through the house.

DING DONG, AND IT'S NOT THE AVON LADY

'I better get that,' John said, stepping away somewhat embarrassedly, leaving Angie to dry away her tears and make herself presentable. As he walked through to the hall John smiled to himself, maybe the reward he hoped for would be coming to him sooner than he thought.

Angie heard voices at the door then a woman appeared in front of John as they walked into the living room.

'Hi. You must be Ina's daughter. Angie, isn't it?'

'Yes. You are?'

'Anne Robertson. I volunteer with the local cancer charity. I was passing and wanted to pass on my condolences. I hadn't known your mother long, but she was a lovely wee woman.'

'This wouldn't be the Ayrshire Cancer Carers would it,' John asked, the name on the piece of paper he was still holding.

Anne turned to him.

'That's right.'

'Why did you get my mother to donate to your charity?' Angie said angrily.

'We didn't get her, she volunteered to give us money because she appreciated the work we did.'

'So, how did you get to know her?' Angie asked blithely.

'We were passed on her name because she had cancer.'

'My mother didn't have cancer!' Angie said, raising her voice angrily.

'Yes she did. She didn't want you to know.'

'No way. You are lying.'

'I am sorry I am the one to be the bearer of bad news, but she was terminal. She only had about two months left to live.'

'John, can you do something about this.'

Then she turned to the visitor.

'John is a policeman,' she said, as if playing a trump card.

'Mrs. Carpenter, I know it must be a shock to you, but I can show you your mother's case notes. It was me that accompanied her to the Beatson when she went to see the cancer specialist.'

Angie rubbed at her brow.

'No way. Mum would have told me. Let me see her case notes?'

'Sure. I have them in my car. I was due to see her today until I heard she had passed. I was passing the house and saw the cars outside, that was why I came in.'

Anne left, leaving a flabbergasted Angie and John staring at each other.

'Do you think this is genuine?'

'If it's not it would be a scam of major proportions. What you need to ask yourself is, would your mother keep a secret like that from you?'

'Yes. No. God, I don't know. For once I wish Terry was here, he would give me a pragmatic view.'

'Well, hopefully I can help. Let's just look at the paperwork and we will take it from there.'

'It couldn't be forged, could it?'

'As I said, it would be an elaborate scam if they went about forging hospital notes.'

Angie sat nervously on the sofa and waited for Anne to return.

The case notes, such as they were, were in a very thin file.

Angie read each page carefully. First was a copy of the letter inviting her to the Beatson for an appointment, dated 5 weeks previously. Written on ink were the names Keith and Anne.

'Who is Keith?'

'One of our volunteers. His wife died from cancer 5 years ago, he has been driving for us since then. You know hospital visits, maybe taking people out for the day if they have no relatives in the area. Doesn't get a penny, or even ask for one.'

Angie suddenly felt rotten, these folk were volunteering to help vulnerable people and she was questioning their scruples. She read on but her mind was made up.

After that there were single pages each noting a visit and what was discussed. The last sheet was a copy of the agreement where her mother pledged a share of her estate to the charity.

When Angie saw the scrawl of her mother's signature she broke down again.

Through the tears she handed the report to John to cast his professional eye over it.

'She did love you, she told me that was why she didn't want you to know about her cancer. We had also spoken to Ayr hospice about your mother going there when she couldn't cope with the house. That was what she wanted, not to be a burden because you had been such a good daughter to her,' Anne said, trying to make Angie feel better.

'If you don't want to donate anything to the charity, just rip the form up.'

'No. Sorry for doubting you but it was such a shock.'

'I know, I will make us all a cup of tea if you want.'

With that, Anne then went through to the kitchen to do just that. She knew where everything was.

By the time tea was ready Angie had calmed and John had done his best in re-assuring her that all was above board.

Over tea, John asked Anne a throwaway question.

'Anne, on Ina's death certificate it said she died of Covid, yet she had cancer. Would that not have been a contributing factor?'

'Nearly all our patients that have passed in the last two years have had their reason for death put down to Covid. The doctors won't explain why.'

That set John thinking. What if the guy in the hi-viz was some kind of serial killer? Was there a new Shipman stalking the streets of Kilwinning, or even further afield, picking old lonely targets and bumping them off? After all the Doctors were quite happy, like in this case, to simply put Covid down as the cause of death. This case seemed to be growing arms and legs and John couldn't have been happier.

'Did she even have Covid?'

Angie nodded her head. 'A couple of weeks before she died I came over to take her to Morrison's for some shopping. We both did a test and hers was positive, so I went and got her shopping.

The thing was, she never even knew she had it. She had her jabs and a booster, that must have helped.'

THERE IS NO FUN IN FUNERAL

Angie and Terry sat alone in the funeral car, slowly driving from the church towards the cemetery. Angie hadn't cried all day which surprised Terry.

'Why did they thank Ayrshire Cancer care? She was always for kid's charities and your dad's heart charity,' Terry asked.

Angie hadn't told him about Anne's revelation. She had felt like a failure to her mum and hadn't been able to tell anybody, even her husband. Now wasn't the ideal time but it had to be done.

'Mum had cancer.'

'What? Your mum had cancer? No way.'

'It's not something I would joke about. The thing is, she didn't want me, us, to know. She kept it a secret. She only had two months to live.'

Terry put a hand over his face. What had he done? Maybe it was an act of mercy, his mother-in-law not having to suffer the indignity of wasting away but right then, it didn't feel like that. It felt like he had ordered her murder for nothing.

The mourners were waiting around the open grave when Terry and Angie walked over.

John was there with wife Karen. As Angie and Terry approached the grave he felt Karen squeeze his arm, it was a signal to him. For some reason after attending funerals Karen was always as horny as a teenager. John was certain he would be on the bones that night. While he was being physical with his wife he knew he would be imagining it was Angie he was bedding.

Since that fleeting kiss at her mother's, bedding Angie was all he fantasised about.

Although they were there for Karen's aunt's funeral John couldn't switch off from the day job. As they waited on the two chief mourners he scanned the crowd. Most were family, meeting for the first time in years, as well as a few neighbours. Anne from the cancer charity was there with another woman, probably another carer. However, one figure stood out. A tall guy, on his own, stood on the fringes, making no social interaction with anybody else. John's interest was piqued.

When Angie stood at the grave and saw the size of the tiny white coffin she finally lost it, crying like a baby. Terry beside her should have been strong for her in that moment but he also burst into tears.

Although she saw the coffin in the church now, above a hole dug for a normal sized coffin, it looked even smaller. Her mother had never been a big woman, but she was losing weight and looked thinner every time Angie saw her. She thought it was just old age but now she knew different.

After a moment Terry managed to stop crying but Angie cried right through the interment. After the minister finished by thanking everybody Terry whispered to her and she managed to compose herself.

They walked away from the graveside and stopped by the funeral car to thank the guests who had turned up to say goodbye to her mother and walked over to speak to her.

There were hugs and cuddles now as friends and relatives were probably meeting for the first time since the Covid restrictions were lifted.

Angie cheered as relatives and friends all said their wee bit about her mum.

Terry, meantime, slipped away from the crowd and met with the guy John had noted as the loner at the back of the crowd. John had been at the opposite side of the crowd but slowly made his way round the edge so he could try to eavesdrop, but they were too far away and spoke very quietly. From the body language, on not too friendly of terms.

After speaking Terry re-joined the group while the other guy headed away, no doubt to get his car.

John waved his car keys towards Karen, who had noticed him going away and wondered why he had left her side, then hurried after the stranger.

As he got nearer he started to get excited, something about the way he walked had the policeman thinking he could be the killer. What, though, was the connection to Terry? Maybe he had killed Ina for Terry. Did Terry know about the cancer and not want her to suffer? It would still be murder; euthanasia was still against the law in Scotland.

Of course, he could still be putting 2 and 2 together and coming up with 22 but you needed a nose for crime to be a good policeman and something about the guy didn't seem right.

The guy suddenly was in a hurry and hightailed it back to his car and quickly drove off.

The guy was too quick for John and was driving through the cemetery gates before he could get close enough to see the car registration. It was a large blue hybrid but that meant nothing, they all looked the same now. However, he managed to pull out his phone and take a quick snap. He looked at it as he got his breath back and saw it was blurry. Back at the station he could get it to the boffins, they would be able to get it cleared up. The problem was it would take time, his whim about a serial killer would put it way down the priorities.

John got in his car and for a moment thought about driving after him. No, he couldn't, he realised. If he drove off and left his wife in the cemetery, in front of her family and some of her friends, his life wouldn't be worth living.

Then another thought came to mind. He switched off the ignition and headed back to the mourners. As he got there they were just starting to break away. Usually there would be a tea afterwards, usually tea and sandwiches, sausage rolls and alcohol if it was in a pub or hotel, but Angie had gone against tradition, she wanted to grieve in her own way.

There were only about 25 folk there all told, hardly enough to lay on a purvey for. Truth was, she didn't think there would even be that many, most of her mother's friends were either dead or in care.

John headed for Angie and Terry. He was arm in arm with Angie but for once it was him he wanted to speak to. Karen was standing nearby, and he signalled for her to go with what he was after. After over thirty years of marriage words were not always necessary.

John shook Angie's hand. It was still shaking to the touch.

'So sorry for your loss,' was all he said, no recognition or giving away their secret quest.

'Thank you, John, isn't it?'

She said it in a way as if she wasn't sure if she got it right.

John smiled and nodded.

As if on cue Karen approached her cousin, just as her husband shook hands with Terry, forcing him to leave his grasp on his wife's arm.

'You must have missed your mother-in-law; you seemed really cut up earlier.'

'Yes. I think it was because it was so sudden.'

Karen had taken his place in front of Angie, and he moved Terry away slightly to have a quiet word.

'Tell me, who was the guy you were talking to. I thought I recognised him.'

'Who?'

'The tall guy, well dressed, stood at the back of the crowd.'

'Oh, Andy Cameron. He is from Kilwinning, he was brought up beside us down the Blacklands. He was my best mate growing up.'

'Is that where you are from?'

'Yes, Kilwinning born and bred.'

'Oh, with you living in Troon I thought you were from down that way.'

'No, like Angie, we are both Kilwinning born and bred. Maybe not something you should own up to.'

'Right, did he know your mother-in-law then?'

'Yes, he told me he was Ina's insurance man many years ago.'

'Where does he live now?'

'I don't know. It's the first time I have seen him in 20 odd years.'

'Andy Cameron, you say. No, I don't know the name. He must have one of those faces that look familiar. They say everybody has a doppelganger.'

'Well, thanks for coming and paying your respects.'

As he turned and went back to wrestle his wife away from her cousin's clutches John felt like laughing. Andy Cameron indeed. There was only one comedian at the funeral, and it wasn't the guy at the back of the crowd.

As they drove away from the cemetery Karen started questioning him about his little production at the graveside. He was left with no choice but to tell her all. Previously he told her he just pacified Angie and paid her lip service as she asked him.

She shivered at the thought that there could have been a killer among them there at the funeral.

Driving home John's mind was in overdrive. Since she had spoken to the cancer woman, Anne, as he now called her, he wondered if there could be somebody out their offering euthanasia services in the knowledge that all deaths were going down as Covid. Under the umbrella of that knowledge he, or she, would be free to knock off people as they wanted.

Karen got out the car when he stopped in their driveway. He told her he would be in after he made a quick phone call.

The desk sergeant on duty at Saltcoats police station, Norrie Johnson, eventually answered the call. John quickly asked if he was on duty the next morning. He was. That was good news for him, he could always rely on a wee favour from Norrie as he knew him from way back when they were both beat cops.

'Looking for a wee favour, Norrie.'

'Right.' The reply was guarded, he had done a few wee favours for John that grew arms and legs, leaving him with more work than he wanted.

'I just need a P.C. for a few hours. Somebody who is computer literate, you know me and the magic box in the corner.'

'Is that all. Really? Nothing more? Are you sure, I know what your wee favours are like?'

'No, really. I want them to look into some statistics for me.'

'Wow, you want to look at statistics. They might make a real detective of you before you retire.'

'Ha bloody ha. Cheers mate, I owe you one.'

'John, go up and get your suit off. It was just dry cleaned; it will do you for another funeral.'

He wasn't happy because he hadn't even got the front door closed behind him when she was dishing out the orders. Still, he knew he would be on a good thing that night.

As ordered John took his suit off and put it back in the suit holder. Just as he put his old chinos on Karen walked in the bedroom.

She was already getting undressed, taking off the black trouser suit.

'Don't bother putting them on, get into bed.'

'But.'

'You know how horny I get after funerals. Come on, let's do it now.'

'But it's day light and we haven't even had our tea yet.'

'Are you knocking me back?'

'No,' he said and whipped the trousers off again.

He lay naked under the covers watching his wife undress. He felt himself harden but only because he was already imagining what it would be like to have sex with Angie. Watching her today, sobbing, vulnerable, he was so jealous of Terry. He probably wouldn't be having sex with her that night, but he got to lie in bed with her.

John lay in bed recovering while beside him Karen sparked up a cigarette.

After she blew a big puff of smoke into the air she reached out a hand and patted his chest.

'What got into you, you were like a man possessed?'

'Really? I didn't think I was any different.'

'Oh, you were. Like a fine wine you are getting better with age.'

'What are we doing for tea then, I am starving,' he said, in his usual passion killer mode.

STATISTICS, STATISTICS AND STATISTICS.

John arrived at the station just after the morning meeting. All night he thought about the prospect of solving Angie's mother's murder. He hadn't slept much and although he had set an earlier alarm, he was up long before it.

He approached Norrie and offered him a thumbs up.

Norrie smiled back. 'Helen,' he called to the office next door.

P.C. Helen Begg appeared round the door.

John's heart sank, it was the Love Island fan. The last thing he needed was an airheaded woman.

Although nobody else would have saw a slight twitch at the side of John's mouth, a sign he was disappointed, Norrie saw it.

'Don't worry, she is our computer whizz,' Norrie said while he patted John on the back reassuringly.

John forced a smile then headed to his office with Helen following. Even walking in front of her, he could smell her heady perfume. In his small ex-cupboard office, it would be overpowering. Hopefully she would get the information he needed quickly.

John let Helen sit behind his computer and fire it up. Watching, John sat opposite the desk in a seat crammed in the other side.

Once she was logged in she looked at him questioningly.

'What is it you are after?'

'Right, I need some statistics.'

He paused before going on as he didn't know how to phrase it. Bull by the horns, just tell her everything.

'Right, before I go on I need your re-assurance this conversation is strictly between us. No gossip at breaktime with your colleagues.'

'Cross my heart and hope to die,' she said with a smile as she crossed her heart with a finger.

'This might sound silly or far-fetched, but I have a theory there might be a serial killer operating in Kilwinning.'

Helen looked at him but never spoke. She didn't need to, her look told him everything.

"Right, I know what you are thinking. The old guy who works in the cupboard has finally flipped. So, here is why I think it. My wife's cousin thought her mother was murdered. I had a wee look into it and found a strange character was near her house. Not much in that you might think. However, the woman was buried yesterday, and a guy was hanging about in the background. I think it was him. I chased after him, but he was in his car and away before I could catch him. I managed to get a photo of his car as he drove away, but the picture is a bit fuzzy.'

'Is it on your phone?'

John nodded then got his phone out and quickly retrieved the snap.

'Have you got a cable to connect your phone to the computer?'

John thought for a moment then went into a filing cabinet and pulled out a bundle of cables. When he handed them to Helen she just shook her head.

After a bit of sorting, she found the right cable and handed the rest back to John, who dumped them back where he found them.

'That's the one,' she said smiling.

She got the picture on screen and blew it up as much as she could.

'No, can't see the reggy plate, but it's a Peugeot 3008 suv, dark blue. Probably need to go to the boffins at headquarters.'

'I know but if I am only going on a hunch it would be well down their list of priorities. They blame all their delays on Covid these days. If you can get me the info I need it will get done faster.'

'Sorry, I can't help you any more with the picture. What else do you need?'

'Well, I was talking to a girl from Ayrshire cancer care, and she told me nobody from Kilwinning who had died at home in the past two years from cancer. All the death certificates listed cause of death as Covid.'

'Are you sure?'

'That was what she told me. It must be some sort of government cover-up or juggling with figures to make them look better or worse. What my theory is, I think is this guy found this out and had free reign to kill as he pleased because if the cancer sufferers are treated like that why would anybody else be different? The doctor comes in, checks they are dead and writes Covid down as cause of death, job done.'

'Why though? Why would somebody want to go about killing people?'

'Why do serial killers kill? Shipman never said why he did it. Even the experts have different theories.'

'What do you want to know then?'

'Does Kilwinning or North Ayrshire have a higher incidence of Covid deaths. In particular are more dying at home, or maybe that is too hard to ascertain.'

Helen was already clicking on the keyboard as she tried to get the information John was after.

'Can I do anything to help?'

'Yes, you could get me a coffee, white, two sugars.'

'Just a plain coffee, no cappuccino or latte or whatever else you get. I am a strictly tea man myself.'

'No, just coffee. I am a just a plain Jane.'

Probably for the first time John looked at her. She was pretty, no, very attractive, nice hair, bumps in all the right places, certainly nothing plain about her, he thought. The uniform didn't help, it hid her vital statistics.

'Best get the coffees,' he said, then quickly left.

John returned with the coffees five minutes later.

'You aren't going to believe this,' Helen greeted him.

'Go on.'

'North Ayrshire is around average, as far as regions go, coming in at around 8.4%. Kilwinning however is running at just under 16%, nearly double the average.'

'You have found that out already, in 5 minutes. Wow.'

'It's all there on the net, you just need to know where to find it.'

'I also checked other North Ayrshire towns and they are less than the average, Dalry 7%, Kilbirnie was 6% and Saltcoats was on the average at 8%.'

'Kilwinning is double the average, that's more than I thought it would be. That's very good work Helen. Do you still think my theory is far-fetched?'

'I never said that,' she said then smiled. 'Okay, maybe I did think it. It seems the old man who lives in the cupboard might not be crazy after all, as you put it.'

'Next, could you type all that information up as a report and I will see the Inspector. He doesn't even know I am working on this, but I need his permission to get work on that picture expedited and to be allowed to work the case.'

'After that?'

'I won't need you after that Helen.'

'Oh, I see. The thing is, I would like to keep on this a bit longer, see if I can dig up anything else. It's got my interest.'

'Sure, I just thought you would want to get back to your colleagues, update them on what's happening on Love Island.'

'What? Oh that. You must have heard me talking about it the other day. The thing is I am a bit of a nerd and not into all that rubbish at all. It's really banal but I have to watch that rubbish like that to appear to fit in with the other officers.'

A nerd, John thought and smiled, nerds didn't look like that when he was at school.

'Look, if you are happy doing this I would love you to keep on it. I told Norrie I would need you for the morning, and if you can dig this up in a few minutes who knows what you can dig up in a couple of hours.'

Helen smiled then turned back to her screen.

PLANNING FOR PORTUGAL

Although it had only been four days since her mother's funeral, Terry was keen to get Angie on board about moving to Portugal but also knew he had to tread carefully, she was still very emotional.

Sunday morning and they sat quietly at the breakfast bar eating breakfast. Cereal. Angie wasn't up to cooking big breakfasts yet.

'How do you fancy eating out today? Lunch, a treat for you.'

'Terry, we haven't even finished breakfast.'

'I know but you like to be organised. What you are wearing, doing your hair and everything else.'

'God, you make me sound like I am high maintenance.'

'No, you get it just right. Your make-up's always on the mark. You should see some of the girls in the office. They come in with it caked on, must be up half the night plastering it on. You don't wear much but it always suits you.'

Angie looked up and smiled. 'That's nice.'

'It's good to see you smile. It's been a hard time these past weeks, but the worst is over.'

'I still have to empty mum's house and get the keys back to the council.'

'Tell you what, I have plenty holidays left, why don't I take a week off from work and I will get it empty, save you having to face going through her stuff.'

Angie reached a hand over and touched his tenderly.

'You would do that for me.'

'I would do anything for you love. Only I can't get this week off, I have too much on, but I will get things sorted and will have the whole of the following week off.'

Terry paid the taxi while Angie headed back into the house. Their Sunday lunch at her favourite restaurant in nearby Loans couldn't have gone better.

Angie had her coat and shoes off and was sitting on the sofa waiting on him. Normally he had his chair while the sofa was her domain.

'Come, sit here.'

Terry joined her.

'I will need to loosen my belt, that was brilliant as usual,' he said before sitting down.

'Yes. I will be back on the diet tomorrow.'

'Diets. You are lovely as you are.'

'Do you still love me; I know I can be hard work at times?'

'Yes I do.'

'Would you still love me if I was old and fat?'

'I said I do.'

They both laughed at his cheek then Angie leaned in and kissed him. Angie was wearing a summer dress and her legs were bare. Terry liked her showing her legs off, but she thought they were too fat and usually wore trousers. As they kissed Terry rubbed his hand over her knee. Her skin was soft to the touch, and he gently moved his hand up her leg.

They broke off the kiss and she moved his hand off.

'Maybe later,' she whispered, even though they were alone in the house.

Terry, buoyed by the three whiskies he had with his meal, decided to take the bull by the horns.

'Do you think we should start planning for Portugal.'

'Yes, a holiday later in the year would be nice.'

'No. I mean planning to move there.'

'Was that your plan all along? Get her giddy with a few vodkas then she would agree to anything.'

'What do you mean anything? Portugal was always our dream. Every time we went there we would say wouldn't it be great to stay.'

'That's just what you say when you are on holiday. Wouldn't it be great to stay here, everybody says it, but it's just talk? You are relaxed when you are away, and everything seems better than back home.'

'Portugal was always our dream.'

'No, it wasn't. It was your dream maybe, but I just went along with it to appease you. I couldn't live abroad.'

'I don't believe you. That's the only thing that's kept me going for years, the thought of waking up every morning with the sun on our faces. No more snow and rain.'

'Well, you go. I will stay here.'

Terry got up and walked over to the drink cabinet.

Angie got up and headed for the lounge door. 'I am off to bed; you are in the spare room if you are drinking any more whisky. I am not listening to you and your snoring tonight.'

MONDAY MORNING BLUES

Terry was rough as a badger's arse. He hadn't made it to bed and ended up drunk on the settee. It was bad enough Angie storming off to bed in a huff but the fact she wasn't interested in moving to Portugal after all the times they had spoken about it made it worse.

The morning shower hadn't sobered him any and when he sneaked into their bedroom to get his gear his wife shouted from beneath the covers that his work suit was in the spare room.

Right at that moment he felt like strangling her himself. By now, after thirty-two years of marriage, he knew how her moods went. Raging first then later that day she would text and apologise, no doubt blame her mother's death for her mood although she always had a reason for her bad behaviour toward him. Truth was, he thought she was just, at times, borderline nutter.

The sun was out early and only a few wispy clouds were in the sky but it wasn't enough to lighten his mood as he walked to the station.

Colin had turned up unannounced at his mother-in-law's funeral and demanded he carry out his half of the bargain. He expected a call but was surprised when he turned on the phone he gave him that morning that there were no new missed calls or text messages.

The train was on time and the platform wasn't busy. Inside the carriage there were plenty of seats and he picked a two-seat job and sat on the outside seat hoping nobody would join him.

After Irvine, the next stop, there were plenty empty seats, so he moved in next to the window and leaned against the side of the carriage, hoping to drift off to sleep, his head still thumping with the whisky hangover.

He drifted off and hadn't noticed the train stop until he felt somebody join him on the seat then spoke quietly.

'Rough are we.'

Even with his eyes closed and the guy speaking quietly he knew who it was. Colin Allardyce. Now he realised why there were no messages on the phone, he had decided to ambush him instead.

'Hangover.'

'You will have more than a sore head if you don't get on with your part of the bargain.'

'Do you know what I found out? My mother-in-law had cancer, she only had two months to live.'

'What's your point?'

'You killed her for nothing. Ironic, isn't it.'

'Ironic or not, I still killed her. Anyway mate, if I hadn't killed her she would have slowly wasted away and died. Imagine sitting with your wife at her bedside watching her mother slowly disintegrate before you. I actually did you a service.'

Colin paused before continuing.

'When I was a teenager I went to see my grandfather at Irvine Central. He had been a farm labourer all his life. A big, strapping mountain of a man, hands like shovels they were, Then, he got cancer. When I went to see him before he died he was only six stone and didn't know who we were, where he was or even who he was. That's what your mother had in front of her, and you would have had to watch her disappear in front of you.'

That brought another, extended silence.

'Sorry, Colin,' Terry said before continuing.

'The thing is you hate your wife. Right now, I don't. I have given it a lot of thought recently and I know I could kill somebody. I thought about it this morning, with my wife but I hated her then. I would need to meet your wife and hate her, think she deserved to die before I could kill her.'

'You know what you are, you are a shite bag.'

'No, I am not. I bet you went to my mother-in-law's and stood outside listening to the telly, on full blast no doubt and thought this deaf old cow deserves to die. Must have been easy, old dear who weighed about 7 stone soaking wet, quick hand over the mouth, and she was away. Your wife wouldn't be so easy to kill, she would put up a real fight, wouldn't she?'

'Right, I will give you the benefit of the doubt but if you meet her you won't like her at all. Tell you what, I am out tomorrow night. You could go round there and say you have an appointment with me to discuss putting all my pensions in one pot. I will leave all my pensions paperwork out and you could look over it while you assess my wife and decide how best to do the business.'

'Right. I need your address.'

Colin handed over a piece of paper he had already prepared.

'When you have memorised it, shred it.'

HELLO MRS. ALLARDYCE

Terry was shaking in his boots. Well, he would have been, but he was wearing Sketchers. As he stood outside the Allardyce's front door and reached for the doorbell he felt like turning and running away. Well, walking away quickly, running was something not in his vocabulary many years since.

All day he had been thinking about this moment. Once he rang the bell or knocked on the door there was no going back. There was nothing else for it, he had to do it.

The ding-dong seemed to echo through the whole house.

Although it was seconds rather than minutes it seemed an age before he heard any other noise in the house. Maybe she was out. After all, although Colin said his wife would be in, how did he know he was telling the truth. How did he know he even had a wife?

Just as he was preparing to turn and leave there was a rattling at the lock inside. The door slipped open a few inches and a face appeared looking furtively out.

'Mrs. Allardyce. I am Terry Carpenter; I am here to see your husband about his pension.'

'He's not in.'

She seemed to slur her words a bit, as if she had been drinking. It might not be early to start drinking at seven o'clock, Terry thought, but not to be tiddly, to say the least. If she had a drink problem like that maybe that was a reason she shouldn't be here, Terry thought, trying to build up a case for killing her.

'We had an appointment for seven o'clock.'

The front door opened a bit more.

'You better come in so that I can phone him. I will be surprised if he answers, he will have his hands full. Wait here.'

Terry stood nervously and in the hallway and watched as Sadie walked a bit unsteadily through to the lounge, presumably to get her phone.

She was wearing a nightdress, too dowdy for somebody her age, and pink slippers with Velcro fastenings. Strange, usually only disabled or infirm wore style like that. Maybe Colin hadn't told him she had a disability, that would be another tick for popping her off.

She returned talking on her mobile, obviously to her husband.

'Yes, well he is here now,' she said, shaking her head as she spoke.

'In your room, right I will get them for him.'

She hung up and made a face, obviously an, I'm pissed off with him look, but Terry thought it was kinda cute. Then he remembered he was there to hate her, to make killing her easier.

'He forgot to let you know he had something, or somebody else on, but he said he left all his pension stuff out.'

Terry waited in the hallway as she went up the stair. He looked up through the open treads on the stairs, watching as she went up, looking for any signs of debility but she seemed steady enough.

What he did see, as he studied her, was that beneath her nightie she wasn't wearing anything else. No pants or thong, he clearly saw her sex. He should have looked away, tried not to stare but he waited until she headed back down and tried to glimpse it again.

He felt his heart race again, this time for another reason, he was getting turned on, not what he was there for at all. In fact, quite the opposite.

Sadie handed him the folder.

'Best come through and have a seat.'

Terry followed and sat on the settee opposite Sadie as she sat in one of the oversized armchairs.

'Do you want a drink?' Sadie asked, as she lifted a wine glass from a table beside her chair and drained the little bit of white wine she had left in it.

Terry felt his hand shake a bit with nerves and thought a small drink could calm him a bit.

'Just a small one, to be sociable. Not too much, I am driving.'

Sadie got up and went through to the kitchen and returned with two full glasses of wine.

Terry sipped a small amount then put it on the floor at his feet.

'Let's have a look at this stuff, then,' he said, opening the file.

In the folder were eight sheets, all from different company pensions. Terry shook his head.

'He should have transferred each of those as soon as he moved jobs. Over the years he would have accumulated a lot more money.'

'It won't make a difference to me; I won't be there to get any of it.'

'Oh, why?'

'Because Colin has a girlfriend. He thinks I don't know but a woman knows. No interest in sex. Look at me, am I that abhorrent you wouldn't want to have sex with me?'

Terry thought it was a rhetorical question but answered it as diplomatically as he could.

'Well, if I was your husband I would still be having sex with you.'

However, he wasn't in the best position to talk. Although he and Angie had sex regularly, the last couple of times he had failed to ejaculate. She said it was fine, but it made him feel less of a man.

'Well, obviously the floozy is better looking than me.'

'Then Colin must be an idiot.'

'Thanks. You know I offered to sell up, split everything but he refused.'

'Oh, when was this?'

'Last month. Do you know what he said to me? He said he earned everything that paid for this house, so I didn't deserve any of it. Prick. Wouldn't let me go out and work, wanted me to be the wee housewife that stayed home and kept house for him. Cooked and cleaned and did all his housework now he resents me for it.'

Last month. Just before they made their little arrangement, Terry thought.

'How does his pension look, just out of interest?'

'Quite healthy. Not as good, as I said earlier that if he had moved them earlier he would have had a substantial amount more.'

'So, when do you plant to retire Terry?' Sadie asked.

'Really, I could retire anytime. My wife and I always planned to move to Portugal when I retired but she just dropped the bombshell that she wants to stay here in Scotland.'

'No way. I would move abroad at the drop of a hat.'

Sadie drank some more wine. Her eyes now looked glassy from the amount of alcohol she had swallowed, obviously a lot more before he turned up.

'Tell you what, why don't you take me? Colin doesn't want me; your wife doesn't want to go abroad. It's easily solved. Swap.'

Terry laughed. 'If only life was that simple.'

Sadie got up, a little unsteadily, then stood in front of him. She pulled the loose material of her nightgown by her sides, showing off the outline of her body, her curves clearly seen and her nipples protruding a little erectly.

'You could be waking up next to this every morning,' she said, smiling tantalisingly.

The smile slipped off her face when she saw Terry wasn't laughing along with her.

She stepped back and fell into her seat with a thump.

'I am sorry, I am just a bit pissed.'

'Oh, it's not you. You have a marvellous body, it's just I have a lot on my mind, my mother-in-law died recently, and my wife and I have been going through a bad time recently.'

'Oh, I am sorry. You didn't need me going on like an idiot.'

'No, as I said, it's not you.'

The problem was, he had to kill her. He had hoped by now he would have detested her, but the opposite was happening, he was warming to her and actually starting to like her.

He had to find out about the issue with her son. Sadie helped by bringing up the subject first.

'You are married, do you have any kids?'

'No. Never managed it. The Doctor's said there was no reason why we couldn't, just never happened.'

'Ow, that's a shame.'

He now had his chance to ask about her gay son, the one she had disowned so cruelly.

'Do you and Colin have any children?'

Sadie's head fell into her hands, and she started sobbing gently. She took a deep breath and composed herself.

'We have a son. Cameron he is called. He doesn't live here in Scotland, he moved to London when he was 18. He is 31now and I haven't seen him since. Colin disowned him because he was gay. Can't even mention his name. I still phone and write to him every week. He writes back but has to send it via my friend Marion who lives across the street.

That's why I am drinking today, it always upsets me when I speak to him. It was worse today because he told me he is getting married in 2 months' time, and he wants me to go down to the ceremony.'

'Why don't you then?' Terry asked. He was angry with Colin for lying. It now made sense to him; Colin did seem to be the homophobic type.

'I can't. I think it best you go,' she said, getting up to show him out.

Before she moved forward she collapsed in tears. Not just crying but seriously breaking her heart tears cascade down her face.

Terry made for the door, thinking it best to leave her. As he reached the lounge door, he felt the tears well up in his own eyes. Crying for the broken relationship of a woman he barely knew and her gay son who he had only heard his name seconds before.

He turned back and walked over and kneeled before her, taking Sadie into his arms.

'Let it all out,' he whispered in her ear.

Almost immediately he felt her body convulse and the tears soak into the shoulder of his shirt. He patted the back of her head gently, while whispering 'there, there.'

He didn't know what else to say.

After a few minutes the weeping subsided. Before they broke clinch Sadie whispered 'thanks,' into his ear.

As they broke apart they looked into each other's eyes. They looked away then turned back and looked deeply into one and other's eyes again.

The kiss that followed was slow and sensual, gently caressing each other's tongues with their own. It built up and each held the other's head as the kissing progressed form sensual to wanton.

When they broke for air Terry went down and nibbled on her neck before heading down and sucking and chewing at her left nipple through the material of her nightie. Sadie responded by pulling the nightie up. He went back to kissing it. When he stopped his kissing she pulled it over her head and threw it to the floor.

Terry continued kissing down her body until he ended up down on his knees before her. Her naked sex was in front of his face. Oral sex was something he had never indulged in but for some reason lust took over and he prodded his tongue forward, hoping he could do it right.

Angie was a fan of sex and active participant but strictly missionary, anything else was perverted by her prude way of thinking.

Whatever he was doing, he was doing something right. Sadie grabbed his head and pushed it forward, wanting more. He kept on, licking and probing with his tongue until he felt a shudder from her body as an orgasm swept through her.

Sadie then took over. She laid him down and pulled his trousers and briefs down. She grabbed his stiffening cock and started licking it.

Terry was ecstatic, he had never in over sixty years had a blow job. Sexually boring Angie didn't approve of that either, thinking it was perverted too. The closest he had come was when Shona MacIntosh had tried one drunken night, out the back of the Kings Arms disco but after she put it in her mouth she gagged and was sick, expelling alcoholic spewings over his new shoes.

Sadie, however, had another plan. She wasn't blowing him off, she was just lubricating him because next she straddled him and fed his now hard cock inside her. Up and down, she went, very slowly.

Terry had never sensations like the ones that now ran through his body.

'Close your eyes,' she whispered, and he did as he was told.

Lying there, he felt her slowly build up speed, moving quicker and quicker until he felt the sensations getting more intense until he erupted inside her.

Sadie climbed off and lay beside him, panting as she tried to get her breath back.

Terry opened his eyes and saw Sadie lying beside him smiling.

'That was amazing,' he said.

'That was nothing,' she said, before kissing him.

Before leaving, Terry took Sadie in his arms.

'It can't end like this. I want to see you again.'

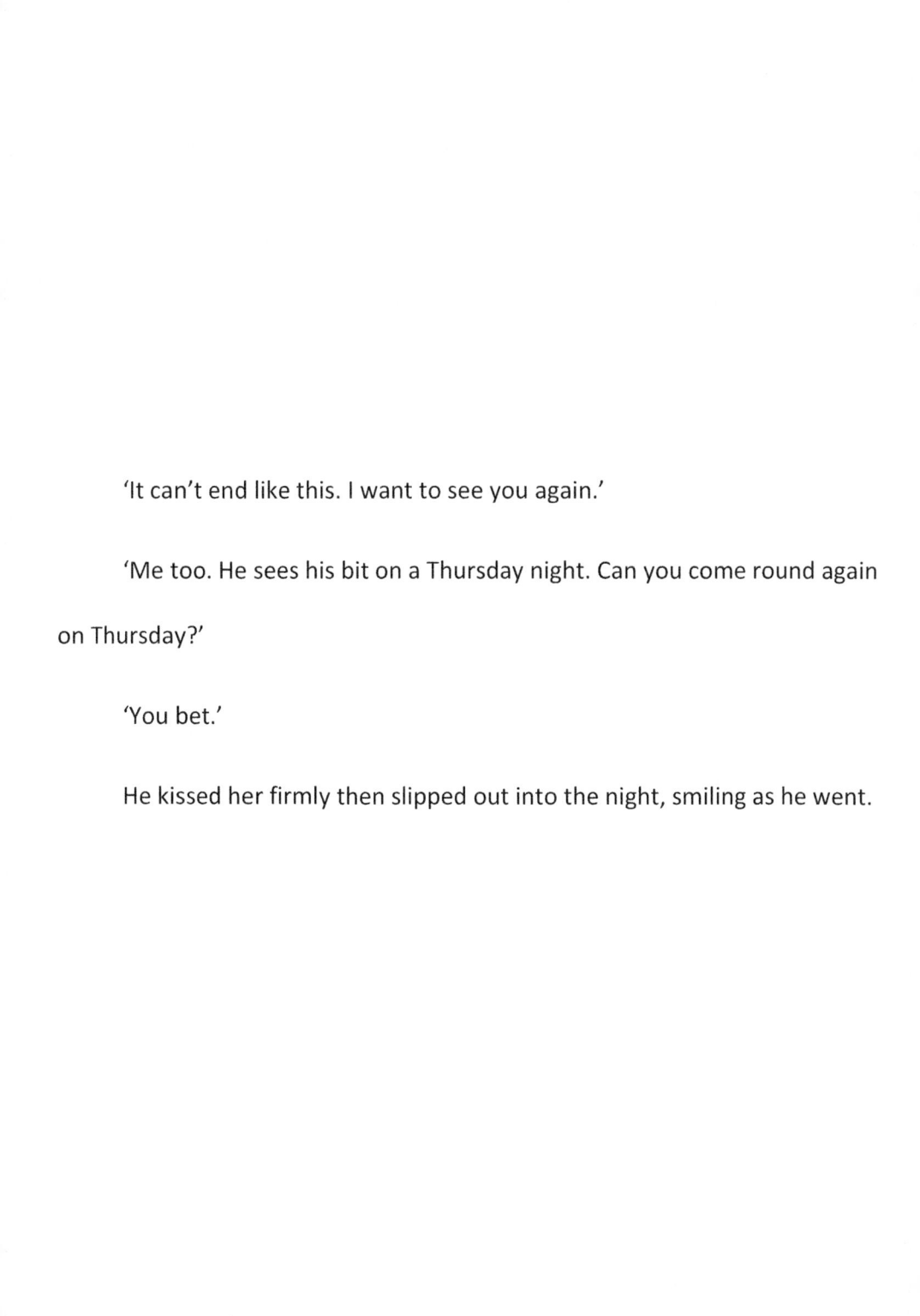

'Me too. He sees his bit on a Thursday night. Can you come round again on Thursday?'

'You bet.'

He kissed her firmly then slipped out into the night, smiling as he went.

DESPERATELY WAITING

D.S. John Rose sat at his desk, desperately waiting on a phone call. He had passed the file that Helen Begg had prepared on the murder of Ina Ralston to his boss, Inspector Kevin Walker, the previous night.

Now, on the Thursday morning, he waited impatiently on his response.

Although he had his computer switched on he just sat staring at the screen, unable to concentrate on any of the cold cases he had still to look over. He knew he couldn't work on anything else until he had spoken to his boss. He needed this case. Not just for his pride but also his sanity, away from sitting in his cupboard of an office day after day. Plus, there was the offer of a special bonus from Angie if he solved it.

When the phone eventually rang, just after eleven o'clock, John nearly jumped out of his skin with the surprise.

'John, I've read the report, I need a word.'

'Just now, sir?'

'Yes, I have five minutes.'

He dropped the phone. It sounded ominous and not positive. His boss was one of the new breed of jumped-up cops, University graduates with all the brains but no police sense, couldn't solve a kids sudoku, never mind a murder case.

John knocked gently on the boss' office door and walked in.

Kevin's office was just like him, neatly turned out, nothing out of place. John's office was never neat as he always had at least three jobs on the go at once and files dumped anywhere and everywhere.

'Very interesting, John. Good work. So, what are you looking for?'

This took him aback. He expected a grilling about why he was working on something that wasn't a cold case.

'Well, I would like to work the case full time. Helen Begg did this report, I would like her working with me, she is very good. Too good to be in uniform.'

'Yes, this is a very good report, very thorough. That's it?'

'Well, the picture of the suspect's car, I would like it pushed through quicker, the car registration would take us to him quickly if he is the person we are looking for.'

'I already contacted head office. They are snowed under and are understaffed with this new wave of Covid.'

'New wave?'

'Yes, they are calling it the New York strain and seems to be spreading a lot quicker. They are down to a skeleton crew up there. Could still be a couple of weeks. Everybody says theirs is priority.'

'We will just need to try from another angle.'

'Right, take this Begg person on board and keep me informed.'

Terry had struggled to concentrate all day at the thought of seeing Sadie again. Angie had mellowed by the Wednesday and was disappointed he had to see the guy about his pension again on the Thursday, she planned it to be a making up night.

That was his excuse for seeing Sadie. The memory of the sexual thrills she had given him had haunted him ever since.

As he drove from Troon to Kilwinning he got a sinking feeling, what if she just screwed him because she was drunk? She didn't have his phone number, she could have regretted it the next day, he could be heading there for a big disappointment.

Terry stopped in his tracks when he rounded the corner where the Allardyce's lived. There were two cars in the drive. Colin was home. He thought for a moment, maybe he wasn't after all, if he was going for a drink, like the first night he met him, he wouldn't be driving.

The desire for more of Sadie had him knocking the door to take a chance. If Colin was in he would say he was there to talk over his pension options. If not, he would find out if the Sadie thing was real or fantasy.

As he stood on the doorstep and rang the bell he suddenly felt like a schoolboy again, hoping his girlfriend would let him pop his cherry after he softened her up with a couple of cider and blackcurrants down the local boozer.

The door opened a crack and Sadie looked out. She looked different; she was sober for one thing and had done her hair and make-up. This time she was wearing a towelling housecoat, a bit more reserved than the last time he was there.

Quickly she opened the door further and ushered him in.

When the door closed he turned and she threw herself at him, kissing him like she had two nights before.

When they stopped kissing she took him by the hand and lead him up the stairs to the bedroom.

Inside she undid her robe showing she was naked beneath it.

'I've prayed all day you would come.'

'I have been dreaming about you since Tuesday night.'

When he dropped his trousers and briefs his cock was jutting out proudly. On the train on the way home, about two hours earlier, he swallowed a Viagra, it's effect now clearly showing.

Terry looked over at the clock. It was nearly ten o'clock. They had stayed in bed for the full three hours since he arrived. All the time they had been having sex and talking in between.

He found it so easy to talk to Sadie, much easier than he could talk to his wife. Although he didn't say it to her, he felt they could have a relationship together. Not some sordid, behind their partners back fling but, even after only knowing her for two nights, he was already thinking they could split up their marriages and go away together. Or was it just the lust for her that was talking to him, thinking with his balls instead of his brain.

'I need to see you again, Terry.'

'Yes. How about you come over to her mother's place on Saturday morning about nine o'clock.'

'Why?'

'Angie has put a thing on Facebook offering her mother's furniture and other stuff for free on Saturday from ten o'clock. I will offer to go over early to start to clear things.'

'Just an hour.'

'It's better than nothing and it's really all I can manage this weekend. I am on holiday next week; I am sure I will manage to see you more next week.'

Sadie kissed him and started stroking his now flaccid coke, which gave a little twitch.

'Don't, I really have to get dressed and go. Anyway, after what we just did there will only be dust left in my balls.'

Sadie laughed then kissed him.

'Till Saturday then,'

WHAT WILL WE CALL HIM?

Friday morning, the day after Walker had given John the go ahead, he stood in front of a whiteboard in a corner of the incident room. Helen Begg was with him, apart from her they were alone in the large room.

'First thing, we need a title up here. What will we call this guy, the Kilwinning killer? Or what about KSK the Kilwinning serial killer. Everybody works in acronyms and initials now,' John asked his new assistant.

'I was thinking, as most of the killings seem to be on a Tuesday night, why not name him the Tuesday night killer.'

Strangely it was a fact more people in Kilwinning died on a Tuesday night than all the others put together. Maybe she was onto something there.

John smiled. 'I like that,' he said and wrote it at the top of the white board with the black highlighter he was holding. THE TUESDAY NIGHT KILLER, he wrote. In bold capitals like that it seemed more official, now they were on a real case.

'Okay, Helen, everybody in the station think I am an old dinosaur. I suppose I am really; compared to you lot, fresh out of police college with fresh ideas but here I hope to show the old one's still work.'

Helen never spoke but looked interested.

'What I use is the five w's. Who, where, what, when and why? Obviously the who, being who did it, is the last one. I once started with the who, but that is another story.'

'First question then is, the why, why was he killing?'

'I have given it a lot of thought, sir.'

'Wow, wow, if you are one of the plebs in uniform you call me sir. When you are on my team it's John or Sarge. Okay.'

'Okay John, well there could be a few of reasons why could have done it. Firstly, it could be to provide euthanasia. If the person has something terminal, say cancer, then it would be better for them to let them go quietly.'

'Good. Secondly?'

'Maybe he takes a fee and kills to order.'

'A sort of assassin?'

'If you want to call it that, yes.'

'Right. Is that it?'

'No. Thirdly there is the actual serial killer angle. Maybe he just likes killing people. If you start killing, and you get away with it you want to try it again and again to show how clever you are. Also, some psychologists reckon they do it for sexual gratification.'

'Really? Get their rocks off because they killed someone?'

'So they say, some kind of weird aphrodisiac.'

'What a strange World we live in. Do you have a fourth suggestion?'

'No. Just the three. So far, anyway.'

'Right, until we get anything back on the car registration we go on these three. We have to establish the next steps for each. If he is providing euthanasia we need to check how many of the dead were terminal. That's my job, Helen.'

Helen smiled back at him ironically. She had the feeling all the next steps would be hers.

'Right, theory two, kill for cash. Once you establish the ones who died who were terminal the others will be favourites for category two. You provide those names, and I will look into them.'

Helen nodded again.

'If anybody doesn't fit into the first two categories, they must be in category three, let's call him the Kilwinning serial killer.'

Helen nodded in agreement, until it dawned on her how much she had signed on for.

John offered to talk again with the staff at the Ayrshire Cancer carers as part of the team's work. He drove to Kilwinning main street where the cancer charity had their shop and headquarters.

The lady behind the counter, although she looked like a female shot putter, looked at him with the kind of distain usually reserved for alkies or druggies.

'Can I help you,' the woman asked, with a voice much deeper in tone than his own.

John swallowed before continuing.

'Are any of the charities administrators here today?'

'Sorry, they are here mainly Monday, Wednesday and Thursdays.'

'Right, I will call back on Monday.'

CLEARANCE DAY

Terry's plan seemed to be working perfectly. Angie had agreed he should go to her mother's house an hour before her, when the clearance of her mother's chattels was due to start. That would give him the best part of an hour to indulge himself.

Sadie arrived just after him. Like a scene from a cheap porno movie, there was a trail of discarded clothes from the front door to the previous occupier's bed. On the bed the lovers fucked like rabbits.

No foreplay or long kissing session, just hot, horny sex.

After twenty minutes they stopped for a break. Terry was glad of the break; his heart was thumping like a big drum of the Orange walk as they passed the chapel on a parade.

They lay there, their limbs still enveloped when a noise outside drew Terry's attention, it was a diesel engine and it sounded like his wife's car.

He jumped up and peered through the curtains. Shit, it was her, more than half an hour early.

'Shit, shit, shit!' Terry said, 'quick, get dressed, my wife is out there.'

The two lovers then jumped about frantically getting dressed, throwing their clothes on as quickly as they could.

Just as the front door handle turned the two were in the hall and respectable again.

'Go with what I say,' Terry said before disappearing into the living room.

'Oh,' Angie said, surprised to find a strange woman standing in the hall.

Terry shouted through, answering for Sadie.

'This is Sandra,' the first name apart from her own that came into his head.

'Hi.'

'Sorry to hear about your mother,' Sadie said in reply.

'Thanks.'

Terry appeared at the living room door with the television in his arms.

'Sandra heard about what you were doing and needs a television. Her son is autistic and smashed his own set. He is lost without it. She wanted to be early because that would be one of the first things to go.'

'Yes, thanks,' Sadie said.

'At least it's going to a good cause. I was scared people would take stuff and sell them on ebay or Facebook.'

'I will carry it out to your car for you,' Terry offered.

'Right, thanks. It's not too heavy, is it.'

'No, not really, I can manage.'

Angie opened the door and Terry walked out with Sadie following.

As they walked over the grass verge Sadie walked by his side.

'What the Hell am I going to do with this,' she hissed. Although they were well out of earshot she didn't want Angie to see them having a cosy chat.

'Take it to the nearest charity shop.'

As Terry sat the telly set on the back seat he saw Angie rushing out towards them.

Oh Christ, he thought, he hadn't removed the sheets, maybe she had seen the damp patch on the bed and worked out what they had been up to.

'Shit, she knows,' he said to Sadie, 'prepare for a scene.'

Angie was panting when she reached them, physical exercise not being a friend of hers.

She leaned out a hand.

'You forgot the remote.'

Terry breathed a sigh of relief.

'Oh, thanks. It wouldn't have been much good without it,' Sadie said.

Sadie got in the car and the married couple stood at the verge, waving her off.

'Where is she from?' Angie asked.

'I'm not sure, local I think.'

'Seems nice.'

Yes, he thought, nice and very accommodating.

First thing back in the house Terry got rid of the evidence, pulling the sheets off the bed and sticking them in a bin bag. They were going to the local recycling centre later that day to be dumped in with the general rubbish.

After 10 o'clock there was a steady stream of folk keen to get something for nothing. By two o'clock the house was nearly empty. In the bedroom there was only the bed left. The lounge was similarly empty except for a wooden chair Angie had brought through from the kitchen. That was going home with her. Every time she would visit her mother she would sit on it, watching her mother making soup or stovies or other good home-made food. This would be something to remember her by.

As Terry ushered the last person out, they were carrying a cheap crappy picture, that Angie would never have given house room and was glad to see it go.

When he went through to the lounge Angie was sitting on the chair, breaking her heart. Everything she had bottled up now gushed out.

Terry rushed over to comfort her.

She stuck a hand out, warning him to keep back.

'Leave me!' she yelled.

Terry stood helplessly and watched as his wife sobbed uncontrollably and her body shook.

'She's gone, Terry.'

'I know. She is at peace.'

'Yes, she is at peace, but I won't be until I know what happened to her.'

'She passed away in her sleep.'

Angie turned with a look of revulsion on her face.

'No, she didn't! Something happened to her in here. You don't believe me, but I know she didn't die peacefully in her sleep.'

Terry looked at her pityingly.

'Don't you dare look at me like that. What is it? Do you think I am mad? Well, not everybody thinks that.'

Angie looked as his expression changed. He looked worried, suddenly she wondered if he had something to do with her mother's death. She had been on the verge of telling him about John Rose and his investigation. He made her change her mind.

Angie stopped crying and dried her eyes.

'What are you on about?'

'Nothing. I told a few of my friends and they knew mum. They agreed she wouldn't have gone to bed with her teeth in. Oh, you don't believe me. Come on, let's get home. Put this chair in your car, I will keep it in the garage.'

MONDAY

Terry got on the usual train on the Monday morning. Since the Saturday afternoon he had been thinking about the incident on that day. Something told him she had talked to another person, not just her friends, about her mother's death. All because Colin had slipped up.

After the train pulled away from Kilwinning Terry was joined by his fellow conspirator.

'Well, you have met her. When are you going to do the business?'

Terry had to stifle a smile, he had already done the business with his wife, on three occasions so far. One thing was for certain, he wasn't going to kill her. Unless he fucked her to death. He had to delay Colin until he worked out what the future for him and Sadie was.

'Something's bothering me. My wife said something on Saturday. I think something is going on with her mother's death.'

'Look, do not think you are wriggling out of this.'

'Wait a minute.'

Terry had raised his voice a bit and looked around to see if anybody was watching them. The usual Monday morning train, people were all plugged in to phones or laptops.

'It was you that fucked up. Putting her in bed.'

'Well, you didn't help by not knowing about the three rings. The phone rang when I was there. I could have rung back but you didn't even know about it. I want you at my house tomorrow night. Without fail.'

'I think Angie has gone to the police. The only reason she let it lie when we found her was because she didn't want her mother getting cut up in a post-mortem.'

'I don't care, I didn't leave any loose leads. Tomorrow night, I want it done.'

Detective Sergeant John Rose arrived at Saltcoats police on the Monday morning with a spring in his step. He had a nice wee case to get his teeth in and an assistant, although not a stunning beauty, who he would readily jump into bed with, given the chance.

It was only a just over a week since Karen and him had sex but his new case had all sorts of hormones running through his body meaning he was already horny as Hell. What drove him on most was the thought of bedding Angie when he solved the case. He was that confident, it wouldn't be if but when.

On the white board in the incident room was a photo of Ina and Angie. John had asked for a photo of Angie's mother but the only one she had was of the two of them together.

John had asked Helen to blow it up to A4 size. He didn't know what it was about her, but Angie had awoken some strange animal lust in him, much stronger than his usual horniness.

Helen arrived again in her uniform. John was disappointed, because not only did it not show off any of her figure she had also opted for a size bigger than she needed. This would be either for comfort or to allow room to grow into. Most cops on the shifts put at least a few pounds on as they struggled to eat normally.

'Helen, you don't need to wear the uniform when you are working with me.'

'Sure, but I feel as if I have more authority in the uniform.'

'Fine, if that's what you like. Did you have a good weekend?'

'Quiet. I studied all the paperwork again and I think I know when the killings started. If there are killings.'

'You still doubt it. If you do you would be better back on the shifts, and I can get somebody that does believe my theory. Until it's proven one way or the other I believe it's true.'

'Sorry, sir, just a bad choice of words. If I didn't believe in it I wouldn't have spent time looking into it.'

'Okay, what is your theory?'

'There were three people died on the first weekend of July, eighteen months ago.'

'Do you have names?'

Helen unfolded a bit of paper.

'James Shedden aged sixty-four, Darren Kelly aged eighty-one and Peter Parker who was seventy-seven.'

'All down as Covid?'

'Yes.'

'Right, I think we need to go to the Kilwinning surgery and speak to someone there. Find out the background on their health.'

'Bags I drive.'

John just shook his head; he was always a willing passenger.

The health centre was busy, and the waiting patients were all wearing masks. John stepped back outside and pulled a mask on. Helen was wearing a black police shroud round her neck and quickly pulled it up over her mouth.

The receptionist wasn't fazed by the police uniform and gave her a look that said, "I don't care what you want, I won't be able to help you."

Helen leaned into the screen, so she didn't have anyone overhearing her.

'I need to speak to somebody about some old health records.'

'The doctors are all busy, you will need to make an appointment.'

Helen bit her lip before continuing.

'What about the health centre manager? Could she help?'

'I doubt it.'

John had joined Helen standing at the counter but left her to it.

'Let's try and find out, eh.'

'I will see if she is available.'

'Thank you,' she said with more than a touch of mendacity.

The receptionist phoned then turned away so that they had no idea how their conversation was going. When she turned round she was wearing a false smile.

'The centre manager is just coming through to see you. Shouldn't be a minute.'

Helen looked at her temporary boss who winked at her cheekily.

From the bowels of the centre the manager appeared. She was in her fifties and looked as if having to walk through the 10 feet or so was already a strain on her obese body.

'This way,' she mouthed and gestured with her hand.

Her office was quite large but there was only one seat on the opposite side of the desk. Helen wanted to stand but John insisted on her sitting. He also gestured for her to do the talking.

'How can I help?'

'We have three suspicious deaths from eighteen months ago. We want to know what was in their health records.'

'I really should have a warrant but if you just want a verbal summary I can do that.'

Helen looked up at her boss who gave her a slight nod confirming it was okay. Helen handed the list that she had already put on the white board back in the incident room.

The manager spoke without even looking at her computer.

'James Shedden. He had Covid and died before the ambulance arrived. The Sheddens went to the local papers and tried to blame us.'

Next, she started tapping with great dexterity on the computer keyboard.

'Darren Kelly was suffering from cancer. He was first diagnosed with it 2 years previously but in the last month his medication was being increased. When he got Covid it was just a matter of time before he passed. According to this he was on very strong painkillers.'

The two police looked across at each other. Sounded positive.

The manager then clicked away again.

'Peter Parker passed away when the doctor was present. Heart attack.'

'Could you give us the address for the Kelly household?'

The manager shook her head gently while she wrote something on the sheet of paper.

'Sorry, but that is more than my job is worth.'

She handed the paper back then got up signalling their time was up then got round to show them out.

'Thanks very much for your time,' Helen said after looking at the piece of paper.

As they walked through the waiting room Helen stopped at the reception window. The snooty receptionist pretended to be busy, but Helen waited patiently until she turned to her.

'Thanks for your help. You have a nice day now,' she said with a smile then walked away.

As they walked back to the car John turned to Helen.

'Good job there. On the old days we would have found out who the snidey bitch on the reception was and would have followed her while she was driving until we could give her a ticket.'

'Sometimes I think the old ways weren't so bad.'

'The manager was okay.'

'That's another thing that bothers me. A woman manager should be a manageress, all this gender stuff does my head in.'

'Well, at least she gave us the Kelly's address.'

'Darren Kelly. Since you mentioned his name it's been bothering me, I am sure I know him. He is the same age as me. If he is originally from Kilwinning he must have been at school with me.'

They got in the car.

'The address is in Waterside Crescent. Are we going there just now?'

'Yes. Let's strike when the iron is hot as they say.'

'So, you are originally from Kilwinning.'

'Yes, born and bred.'

John clicked his fingers.

'It's big Daz. He was never called Darren, well not by us. Ever since he started school he was called Daz. It was one of those ironic nicknames because his family weren't the cleanest.'

'Big Daz. Was he a big guy?'

'Yes, he was the school bully, well the bully for our year. Now he's dead, good riddance.'

Helen knew the way to Waterside Crescent, it was an area the police visited on a regular basis, especially at the weekends.

Waterside was in a typical council housing estate street in Kilwinning, or any other town in Ayrshire. There was a mixture of bought houses, pimped and well looked after and others that were still lived in by council tenants most of which were lived in and little more. Living in them a mixture of mostly honest, law-abiding citizens and some of the opposite.

The Kelly's house was one of the latter. The front grass long enough to graze sheep in. One of the upstairs windows was taped up with cardboard over a crack in the glass.

They were welcomed by next door's devil dog, tied out the back door to a clothes pole that barked and strained its tether in its desire to rip them apart.

'Softly, softly, here,' John cautioned, as they stood on the doorstep. 'Let me do the talking this time.'

Helen knocked gently on the door.

The tenant, Ma Kelly, opened the door then frowned.

'What now?'

'Hello Ma. Remember me, John Rose. Kathy Rose's boy.'

Ma smiled as she remembered his mother, then remembered he was still one of them, a pig, and drew him a nasty look.

'We are looking into the time when your husband passed away. Mind if we come in.'

Myra Kelly walked into her house leaving the front door open for the police to follow.

The living room wasn't just tidy it was spotless, but the décor was gauche. All black, white and grey, a colour snap would have looked like a black and white picture.

Ma sat on one of the oversized chairs while the cops sat together on the luxurious black leather sofa.

'So, Ma, what can you tell me about the night Darren died?'

'I don't know, I wasn't here.'

The cops looked at each other but said nothing. They knew Ma would fill the silence.

'I was at his brother's house.'

As the two on the sofa wondered why she was there, thinking it couldn't have been for what they were thinking, could it?

Myra made a face that said, it's none of your business.

'He lost his wife last year and Darren had been bedridden for six months. Life goes on,' she said, matter of factly. 'It's not against the law, is it?'

'Was Darren here on his own?'

'No, the man was dying for fucks sake. Do you think we are heathens? We took turns staying overnight with him. The night he died our Ed was staying here.'

Edward Kelly, that was a name John knew all too well. Mostly breaking and entering when he was a teenager and John was still a cop on the beat.

'Is Edward keeping his nose clean now?' he asked.

Myra looked as if she didn't know what the D.S. was talking about then she remembered.

'John, he was just a daft boy then. He has a family and a job now.'

They were interrupted by the front door opening and somebody rushing in. Suddenly the aforementioned wild child appeared before them and not happy to see the 2 cops on the couch.

Edward Kelly stood about six foot tall and was well at himself, an imposing figure of a man.

Straight away John thought he resembled the guy from the graveyard. He couldn't see too well without his glasses on that day and he was a fair distance away but he looked about the right size.

'Tell them nothing mother!'

'Edward, don't shout at your mother.'

'Sorry mum,' he said, bowing his head.

'They are just asking about the night your father died.'

'We were coming to see you next,' the detective said.

Edward put his hands on his head

'God, can you not leave us in peace. Is it because he died of Covid, and it was me that gave him it? Is that a crime, did I kill him?'

It looked as if Edward thought he was guilty of killing his father and had carried the blame since then.

'Was it just you at his bedside when he passed away?' Helen asked. Her voice quiet and caring.

Tears now racked the big man's body. He couldn't talk and just nodded.

They others sat in silence until the big man could control himself.

'Yes, it was just me. I had Covid too. I knew he was going to die that night but didn't want the rest of the family getting ill because of me.'

John got up and Helen followed.

'We will leave it at that,' he said.

As he walked past Edward John stopped and patted him on the shoulder.

'He was a good man, your dad. Everyone in the area looked up to him.'

Edward nodded his appreciation as the 2 police edged past.

As they drove off in the car John spoke first.

'What are you doing tomorrow night?'

Helen waited until he expanded before she answered.

'I'm not offering you a date; I am going to watch our friend Edward Kelly tomorrow night. See if he has any nocturnal pastimes that might interest us. Fancy coming along for the ride?'

'Sure. But does that mean we will work all day then follow him at night?'

'No, we will do a backshift, start at two and finish at ten unless we hit it lucky, and he is the Tuesday night killer.'

TUESDAY

Tuesday night and Terry drove to Sadie and Colin's house. Long before he laid eyes on Sadie he had planned how he would kill her. He couldn't strangle her, he knew that. Stabbing would be too messy, a guy walking through the streets with bloody on his clothes would arouse suspicions, no he had decided he would use a rope. Make a noose, slip it over her head from behind and pull it until she stopped moving. Sounded simple when he thought of it like that.

Driving that night, he had no rope or other strap to choke her with. In fact, although he had all but promised Colin he would do the deed that night, the deed he hoped he would be doing was of a sexual nature.

Unless, of course, Sadie's ardour had cooled towards him. It might do later because tonight he planned to tell her about his agreement with her husband. God knows how she would take it.

When he knocked gently on the front door it opened invisibly, letting him walk in. Looking behind the door he found Sadie standing there as naked as the day she was born.

With her right hand she pushed the door closed behind him. When he turned he didn't get a chance to look surprised, Sadie was all over him like a rash. Kissing, grabbing, trying to get his clothes off.

Terry quickly got with the program, reaching for her erogenous zones while trying to join her in nakedness.

They never even tried to go up the stairs to bed for comfort, they screwed right there, on the hall floor.

On the train home, a few hours earlier, Terry had swallowed a Viagra. Once wasn't enough for Sadie, she had been insatiable. The blue pill had him ram rod hard even after he had ejaculated for the first time there.

Afterwards they lay on the floor recovering, the coldness of the parquet floor not bothering them, in fact helping with the healing.

'Put your housecoat on, there is something I need to tell you.'

'Sounds ominous.'

'There is something important I want to ask you, but I need to tell you something else that's even more important first. If you were sitting naked I couldn't concentrate on what I have to tell you, I would just want to keep touching you.'

Sadie disappeared up to the bathroom upstairs to tidy up and get something on as asked.

Terry pulled his clothes on then went through to the lounge then started pacing while he waited on her return.

Sadie walked into the lounge to join him. She was wearing a short negligee that had most of her legs out on show.

Terry felt himself start to harden again; such was the power of the blue pill. He felt guilty for lusting after her because he might just be about to break her heart.

'Sit down,' he asked.

Sadie went to sit on the sofa, but Terry asked her to join him at the dining room table, where he sat opposite her.

'I want to ask you to leave Colin and come to Portugal to live with me.'

Sadie's eyes lit up and she opened her mouth to speak. Terry quickly leaned over the table and put a finger gently to her lips to stop her speaking.

She kissed it gently making him pull it away.

'I met your husband Colin on a train back from Glasgow one Friday night about six weeks ago. We were both drunk and spoke about our lives and what would make them better.

I said if my mother-in-law was dead I could move to Portugal. He said if you were dead he could move in with his girlfriend.'

'Cheeky,' she started miscalling her husband, but Terry stopped her.

'Oh, he painted a very different picture of you to the one I met. A drunken sot who sat about doing nothing all day. He also said you didn't want anything to do with your son because he was gay and he couldn't give you any grandchildren.'

Sadie's eyes were starting to pop out with what Terry was saying as her anger grew. Terry signalled to let him continue.

'I am not proud to say it now, but I agreed with Colin if he killed my mother-in-law I would kill you.'

'He killed your mother-in-law. How? When?'

'About a month ago. He went into her house and smothered her.'

'Oh my God, I can't believe this. Get me a drink.'

Terry went over to the drinks cabinet but could hardly pour her a vodka because his hand was shaking so much.

'The irony of the thing is, Ina, my mother-in-law, had cancer and only had a couple of months to live. Added to that now my wife won't move to Portugal with me and never planned to live abroad, so it was all for nothing.'

Sadie had greedily swallowed half of her vodka before she had a thought.

'This isn't drugged, is it?' she asked, holding the glass of spirits out as if it was poison.

'No. I told you Colin painted a very different picture of you. That wasn't the lovely, caring woman I found. The woman I have fallen in love with. I could never harm a hair on your head far less kill you.'

'He hates me so much he wants me dead. I could kill him!'

The couple held hands across the table.

'The question I said I would ask you earlier, will you come to Portugal and live with me. Well, I am asking you now. Will you?'

Terry hit Colin's number on the pay as you go phone he had supplied. He felt his hand shake nervously. It seemed to ring for ages before Colin answered. There was a lot of noise in the background, he was obviously in a pub getting his alibi sorted.

'Why are you phoning? Is it done?'

'You need to get back here quickly.'

'What? I can hardly hear you.'

'Get back here quickly!'

There was a pause then the phone went quiet, obviously Colin had his hand over the phone.

'I can't get back until about half past nine.'

'Okay, I will be waiting.'

John Rose and Helen Begg sat in the unmarked police car along the street from Edward Kelly's house. Although it was unmarked, everybody knew the detectives in North Ayrshire drove dark blue or black Ford Focus's.

Helen had taken her boss's advice and wore casual clothes, wanting to feel part of the team, all be it a two-person team.

John welcomed the change in dress. Her tight jeans showed off a very sexy arse but unfortunately her tight top showed a distinct lack of breast. John had always been a big breast man but wouldn't let that stop him if Helen offered him any extra-marital services. Business first, they had Edward to follow.

It was a dry evening which helped, the windows wouldn't steam up. They had been there since before nine o'clock and were staring to get uncomfortable in the heat.

There was a car in Edward's driveway, a dark blue Peugeot, the kind of car from the graveyard, so they assumed he was in the house.

John kept a lookout on the house the whole time they were there while his driver spent much of the time on her phone. The phone addicted young people really did his nut in, probably just an age thing he thought but he wondered what they did all the years before they were invented.

'Oh oh, action,' John said.

Edward was on the move, he had opened the boot of his car and put a hi-viz jacket and bag inside.

'Don't start the car yet. If he hears the noise it might draw his attention.'

Helen waited until she saw the reverse lights come on as he prepared to come out of his driveway before firing the Ford's engine.

'Have you followed a car before?'

'No.'

Jesus Christ, John thought, why did he not think to ask before.

'Well, now you will learn. You need to keep far enough back so that he doesn't clock you while making sure you don't lose him. Like at the lights on the way out of the estate.

Edward lived in the same council scheme as his mum although at the opposite end. He was heading up and out of the estate. As John had warned there were a set of lights and Edward was stopped by a red light.

Helen pulled up behind him but left a bit of room.

When the lights changed they were surprised when he turned right, heading out of the town.

'Maybe he is branching out,' John said, as the quarry drove past the last houses in Kilwinning, heading for the next town, Dalry.

'Wonder if he has clocked us?' John mused, as Edward was driving very slowly and carefully.

'Maybe trying not to arouse any suspicion,' Helen replied.

'Good thinking, lass.'

They followed the car right through Dalry, the next town and it seemed to be heading for Kilbirnie, the town after that. However, just on the outskirts of Dalry, he turned off and into a large factory car park.

'Keep back, he might have seen us and be going to drive round the car park to catch us.'

Just then another car approaching from the other direction started indicating they were going into the car park.

'Right, Helen, let him go in first then follow them in.'

By the time they got into the car park Edward was already parked up but was still sitting in his car.

Helen parked about three rows behind him, near enough to keep him in view but far enough to not raise suspicion, then she killed the engine.

'What do you think, Sarge?'

'There a couple of bungalows just across the road, maybe he is going there. Of course, he could be walking back to the housing estate further back.

If he has got away with murder for so long he could be getting really cocky. Another thing, they say you become invisible when you wear hi-viz.'

Edward got out of the car, as he did so it sent the adrenalin rushing in the two cops who were watching him.

'He is on the move, what's the plan, sir?'

'Well, he knows me, I can't follow. You will need to get out and shadow him.'

'But he saw me on Monday.'

'Yes but on Monday he saw a police officer, you are certainly in plain clothes now. '

As Helen unclipped her seatbelt Edward had already popped on his hi-viz jacket and was walking through the car park.

'Turn your radio down in case you get a message, and he hears it. He is a bit handy with his fists as I remember.'

John struggled to see what was on the back of his jacket. There was black writing but once again he wore his contact lenses and struggled a bit without his glasses.

Before he could ask his colleague what it said she was already out and walking away from the car.

As she walked slowly toward Edward, John realised they had wasted the evening, he was going into the factory. It must say security on his jacket.

When Helen re-joined him he burst out laughing.

'Why did you not follow him in, you might have got a nightshift.'

Helen joined in, laughing, before saying, 'we haven't proven it's not him, just because he won't be able to kill somebody tonight doesn't mean he isn't guilty. Even serial killers need to earn a crust.'

'Come on, drive us back to headquarters.'

Colin opened the front door and walked slowly into the lounge. His wife Sadie was propped up in her chair, looking devoid of life. Terry stood behind the chair looking grim.

'Have you done it? Why are you still hanging about here?' Colin asked, amazed he had actually carried the deed out.

He nearly jumped out of his skin when Sadie suddenly jumped up and opened her eyes then pointed angrily at him.

'No, he didn't do it. He is more of a man than you.'

Colin then turned to Terry, anger distorting his good looks.

'What the fuck is going on here?'

'Well, Colin, you described your wife here as some evil old crone. When I met her I found out she was the exact opposite. To tell you the truth, we are in love.'

'Love. What the fuck are you going on about?'

He leaned a hand down and Sadie took it in hers lovingly.

'More than that, we have a deal for you, seeing as money means more to you than your wife's life.'

'Deal. You have a fucking cheek, you reneged on the last deal.'

'Lucky for you, bastard.' Sadie chipped in, still raging at what Terry had confessed earlier.

'Sadie has agreed she will walk away leaving you with the house, all your money and your pensions, she doesn't want a single thing from you.'

Colin's eyes lit up at the prospect of being free to move his lover in. Then realised there needed to be a massive snag, the offer was too good to be true.

'Hit me with it, what's my end of the deal?'

'I want you to kill my wife.'

'What? Your wife?'

'Yes, you heard me right; you should realise what it means because you asked me to do it for you.'

Colin sat down in his armchair as he digested what had been said.

'How do I know I am not being set up?'

'Sadie will sign everything over to you. You contact your lawyer to draw up the papers and she will sign them. The sooner the better as far as we are concerned.'

Colin looked at his wife for her reaction.

'It's more than you deserve but it's worth it to be rid of you,' Sadie spat at him.

Colin put a hand to his mouth as he thought about it.

'What is there to think about man? Winner winner, chicken dinner,' Terry said.

'Right, I will do it.'

Sadie got up from the chair and rushed round to Terry to seal it with a kiss.

Colin walked over to the drink cabinet and poured himself a scotch.

Sadie wanted the last word. 'From now on you are in the spare room.'

D.N.A. – DON'T KNOW ANYONE

John checked his emails first thing. There was one with the DNA result of the swabs he took from Ina Ralston's bathroom and her hairbrush.

'Helen, what do you make of this?'

Helen walked round and stood over him. She smelled good enough to eat. John was feeling frustrated as it was weeks now since the funeral, the last had sex.

'There is no DNA of the owner in the bathroom but the DNA they have doesn't match anything on the police database,' Helen read.

'What do you think?' he said, hoping to teach her to think the way he did.

'Somebody, the murderer if there was one, used the sink then wiped it down.'

'Yes, that's what I think. Of course, we will need to rule out anybody else who was in the house. I will phone her daughter and get swabs from her and anybody else who might have been in the house.'

John clicked his fingers.

'Helen, could you check and see if Edward Kelly is on the database, see if he has given a DNA sample at some time in the past.'

Helen returned to her computer.

'Bad news, sir, he is on it so, does that rule him out?'

'I'm afraid it looks like it. Our wee trip the other night looks to have been a wild goose chase.'

'It wasn't all a waste of time. You gave me some good tips about how to follow somebody.'

'That's what I am here for. Better phone Angie, follow that lead.'

John felt excitement growing as the phone was ringing.

'Hello.'

'Hi Angie, it's John Rose here, just phoning with a wee update on your mum's case.'

'Right. Is it good news?'

'It could be. We got a DNA result and it showed none of your mum's DNA but there was other DNA on it. So, we need to check on anybody who might have been in the house on the Tuesday.'

'I was in there on Tuesday morning, and I used the toilet but that was before ten o'clock. Mum must have used it after that.'

'I would think so, but maybe it's best we submit your DNA. Will you be in today?'

'Yes, I have been out, no plans to go out again later.'

'Right, I will be over about two o'clock.'

'What if your wife calls your office this morning?'

Terry was playing truant from his work, phoned in sick, and headed to Sadie's as arranged. They were lying in bed, resting.

'Angie? No, she would just message my mobile. In all the time I have worked there she has never phoned the office. Probably hasn't the office number. All these years I had the perfect wife for having an affair but never used it until now.'

He cuddled Sadie again and stroked her inner thigh causing her to giggle.

'You aren't ready to go again, are you?'

'What, after that last performance? No, give me half an hour.'

'We will need to watch the time; I have an appointment at our lawyers at one o'clock.'

'Okay, I will try and be quick.'

'What will you do this afternoon?'

'I will just go home; tell her I felt a migraine coming on.'

As John stood on the doorstep of Angie's door he felt butterflies in his stomach. He prayed she was wearing something low-cut to give him a view of her lovely breasts.

His dream bubble burst when her husband answered the door to him.

'Hi, Terry isn't it.'

Terry looked blankly at him.

'It's John Rose. I am married to your wife's cousin, Karen.'

'Right, got you now. You were at the funeral. Is something wrong with Karen?'

'No, I am here on business I am afraid. You see I am here in my capacity as Detective Sergeant and came to see Angie. I phoned earlier and asked her if she would supply a DNA sample.'

'Oh, well, you better come in.'

As John walked past, Terry wondered what it was about.

'What's this for?' he asked, as if just making conversation.

John was thinking quickly, Angie didn't want her husband to know what they were doing, for whatever reason.

'I work the cold cases, but I also get spot check work. Basically, I am checking that the P.C.'s are doing their jobs correctly. When your mother-in-law died they did some swabs in the toilet and unknown DNA result was found. It's probably Angie's because she was in the house in the morning.'

'Do you do that? Sort of quality control on your own work?'

'Yes. As I said I mainly do cold case work which means I don't have daily contact with the other police officers, so I am free to check their work. This is completely routine, but they should have done this at the time.'

'Right, you learn something every day.'

Angie was sitting in the living room but had obviously heard the conversation in the hall.

'Hi, John. Am I okay sitting here, or do I need to stand up or anything?'

'No, you are fine there.'

As he had hoped for she was wearing a low-cut top and the top of her puppies clearly on view.

John took the DNA kit out and took out the swab stick.

'Just open wide,' he said.

John gently rubbed the swab inside her mouth, his eyes feasting on the delights below as he did so.

Job complete, he put the stick into the collection tub and stuck a label with her name on it.

'So, how long have you been doing this kind of work, John?'

'Just since lockdown. They took a lot of officers away from internal affairs to backfill for shortages. As I am heading to retirement they put me on the cold cases they had from years ago then this work came up.'

There was an embarrassing pause after he answered as Angie and John were scared to say too much and give the game away that they were better acquainted than they should be, and Terry just wanted him out of the house.

'Well, I better be getting on. Crime doesn't solve itself, as they say.'

John headed out, shown out by Angie.

'I will be in touch,' John whispered.

As he left to drive back to Saltcoats he knew his first stop would be the first empty lay-by to relieve himself. It was strange but Angie created urges in him that no other woman could, even his wife.

When Angie walked back through Terry was smiling.

'What?'

'He is a bit of a fish.'

'John. He seems nice enough. Anyway, our Karen wouldn't be with him if he was weird. Are you okay, you look tired?'

No wonder he was tired, he had been romping with Sadie for three hours that morning.

'It's just my head is still a bit fuzzy.'

'You know it will be worse if it becomes a full-blown migraine. Off you go, up to your bed.'

'Maybe you are right.'

'I could come up and join you in a couple of hours. It's been a wee while since we, you know, had a cuddle and stuff.'

'No, really, I couldn't. I am wiped out. Oh, by the way, remember I am at a course in Edinburgh next Monday and Tuesday.'

'What course?'

'Health and safety or something. I told you about it ages ago.'

'How many times have I told you, put it on the calendar.'

'Anyway, after two days away I will be desperate for you. We will have a date night on the Wednesday.'

'All weekend without it. I am beginning to think you have a girlfriend.'

'No, way, love.'

'Well, I hope it's not a boyfriend.'

'You are the only one for me. Right, I am off to bed, see you in a couple of hours.'

BYE BYE ANGIE

Detective Sergeant John Rose and P.C. Helen Begg arrived for work on the Tuesday morning hoping something would turn up. Their immediate boss Inspector Walker had given them a deadline to show some progress by the end of the week or they were back to normal duties the following Monday.

Although they hated being hassled, he sent an email off to headquarters to find out if they had an ident for the fuzzy number plate photo he sent them weeks ago.

They had been checking all the people that had passed away from Covid during the past eighteen months, but it was an endless task, and they were drawing blank after blank. They needed a break and quick if they were to continue.

Terry called Colin's pay as you go phone. He was surprised when it rang.

'What?'

'I am in Edinburgh. Tonight, must be the night.'

'Yes, you said. Your woman reminded me this morning before I went to work.'

'Do you remember where I told you to park?'

'Listen, dum-dum, I am the one who has done this before. You have a cheek trying to tell me what to do.'

Before Terry could reply the phone went dead.

In a way Terry felt sick to the stomach at the thought of his wife of all those years being killed, but the rewards would be worth it.

Just before he switched his computer off for the night, John got an alert that he had a new email. He was going to leave it until the next day, but curiosity made him look.

It was the reply he had waited for all day, it simply was headed regards but the picture, when he opened it was a clear image of the car from the graveyard and the registration plate plainly visible.

'We've got him!'

His sudden outburst gave Helen, who was still opposite him on her computer, a bit of a shock.

'Got who?'

'The Tuesday night killer.'

Helen rushed round from her desk. After looking at the picture she went back to her desk and put the plate ident into the DVLA database to find the identity of the owner of the car.

'It belongs to a Colin Allardyce. The address is in Kilwinning.'

'Right. I don't think we should go rushing over there. Why don't we go home, have something to eat and meet back here at, what, eight o'clock? After all, it's Tuesday night. He might have a wee date with somebody, wouldn't it be nice to play gooseberry.'

Helen smiled. She agreed, it would be great to catch him going prepared.

John checked his phone before starting the drive home to Irvine from Saltcoats. He had a call that he was desperate to make.

As he drove out the secured car park behind the police station he hit the number on his hands-free service.

'Hello.'

'Hi, Angie, it's John.'

He hoped she didn't say John who, he wanted to be the main John in her life.

'Oh, right. Good news I hope.'

'Right, what I am about to tell you is between us and no-one else. Okay.'

'Okay.'

'This is an ongoing investigation, and I shouldn't be telling you or anyone else. It's only because of our special relationship that I am telling you. Understand?'

'Yes,' she said, excitement growing in her voice.

'We have a positive lead on the person who visited your mother's house the night she died. It's a local guy from Kilwinning. Understand?'

'Yes.'

'We are planning on taking him into custody tonight.'

'Wow. That's great news.'

'I will keep you informed. Look, I need to go, I am driving, catch you later. Bye.'

'Bye John, and thanks.'

Angie watched the call go dead then punched the air.

'I was right. Terry thought I was stupid. Those useless plods just wanted me not to rock the boat, but I knew,' she said to herself smugly.

She walked through to the kitchen to put the kettle on but then had another thought. Time to tell him who was right. She settled on her recliner chair then dialled her hubby's mobile.

It rang out, eventually going to his answering machine.

'Terry, it's Ang. Call me as soon as you get this.'

As she waited all kinds of thought went through her head, imagining her husband standing at the bar, drunk at five o'clock or lying in bed with one of the women from the course. She had heard about these kinds of conference.

Angie jumped when her phone rang again. Hubby flashed on the screen. It had taken him more than two hours to finally get back to her. During that time, she had just got angrier with him.

'Hi, love. Sorry, I was in the shower.'

'For two hours, that's as bad as Patrick Duffy?'

'Who?'

'Patrick Duffy, Dallas. Never mind.'

'Sorry, but the conference ran on.'

'Were you alone in there?'

'Where, in the shower? Of, course I was alone. What is so urgent, anyway?'

Angie took a breath and composed herself.

'Remember when my mother died and I said something wasn't right, well I was right.'

'What are you talking about? Have you been drinking?'

'No. Have you?'

'No, not yet.'

'Anyway, John Rose, you know the policeman you said was a bit of a fish, well, he solved the case and is going to arrest the guy tonight.'

'What is this about? Is this because he was over the other day?'

'No. He has been working on this since mum died. I called Karen and she got him to speak to me and he agreed with me that something seemed dodgy.'

Terry felt sick. You need to keep cool, he reasoned. It might be somebody else they were after.

'Who is he going to arrest?'

'He never said exactly, just that it was a local Kilwinning man.'

The phone went dead, Terry hung up. Terry had a terrible feeling in the pit of his stomach that it was Colin they were after. How the cop found out he didn't know, but right now he had to assume it was him and he had to call him off, the hit on his wife had to be cancelled.

Terry thought for a second. He had to contact Colin but the pay as you go phone, the only way he had to contact him, was hidden under the passenger seat of his car. He would call Sadie first, he had her number listed under Barry, badminton, a sport he still played occasionally.

'Shit!,' he said when it went to her answering machine. 'Call me!' he shouted into it.

He would need to phone Colin on the pay as you go, he better have it switched on, he thought. Terry was starting to panic as the implications dawned on him, if Colin went down he would certainly take him with him.

He hadn't dressed since his shower and only had a towel wrapped round his waist. He threw it off and grabbed at his clothes. He didn't even think about clean clothes from his case but picked the ones he threw on the floor and started throwing them on.

He grabbed all his things and threw them in his case and headed out to his car. Going through reception he got a look because he didn't check-out, but he hoped he would only be going out to phone and be back soon, or later that night if he got the whole thing wrong.

Throwing the case on the front seat he reached below and found the secret phone. He switched it on and as soon as he could and hit the only number in it, Colin's. It also went straight to answer machine. Somehow, he expected it would.

His only other way to contact him was to drive back to Troon and intercept him. When he started the engine the clock showed it was just after half past seven. Ninety minutes to get back. It would be tight, but he couldn't break any speed limits, the last thing he needed was to get stopped by the police.

John arrived in the office before eight o'clock, fifteen minutes early and found an eager Helen already there.

'Have you checked out where our man lives?'

'Yes. In the estate just before you leave the town to head to Dalry.'

'Right, let's get over there and see if he has any plans for tonight. Do you want me to drive?'

'Maybe best you do, we could have a chase on our hands. Although I have done the Advanced driving I've never used it in practice.'

John took the keys from her. She was probably right; this could end up a life-or-death situation.

Just as they turned into the estate where Colin Allardyce lived a dark, blue 4x4 turned out past them.

'That's him,' Helen said, recognising the registration, just before John did.

He quickly turned and headed off in pursuit.

The big saloon drove straight through town and onto the bypass with the cop car following at a safe distance behind.

'Where do you think he is off too?'

'Could be anywhere from here. Irvine, Kilmarnock, Ayr, Troon. We just need to follow and see where he goes.'

They tailed him for over 6 miles. At the end of the first section of bypass he went all the way round the roundabout and took the turn off for Troon.

'Looks like he is going up in the world,' Helen said, hinting that they were heading for a town a lot wealthier than the one they left. Troon was one of the wealthiest towns in Scotland.

Terry made it to the spot where he told Colin to park up. He had already checked the area out, ensuring there were no CCTV cameras near there.

All the way there he had been trying to contact both Colin and Sadie, but both numbers continued to ring out. Every mile he drove he regretted everything. Regretted meeting Colin regretted agreeing to his deadly deal. Sure. he didn't regret the sex with Sadie but what had he thinking about by asking Colin to kill his wife so he could live in the sun with Sadie.

Like the bisto kid who only wanted meat, Sadie and he only wanted the sex. What if they moved in together and found out to their horror they couldn't stand each?

By the same token what would happen between them when she didn't want sex as much as him, or he, God forgive, he went off sex himself. They might end up hating each other. Then they would be miles from Scotland and stuck with each other.

Terry drove back the way he came hoping to meet Colin heading the opposite way. When he reached the outskirts of the town he turned and went back the opposite way again.

John and Helen followed the blue Peugeot through the town and parked up opposite where it was parked up. They watched as he reached into the boot of his car and pulled out a hi-viz jacket and hard hat.

'Bingo!' John shouted. 'I knew it was him, that's the guy from the photo. Better get some back-up.'

Helen went straight on her radio. Although technically they were out with their own area they knew they would get instant help from the locals.

Colin was dressed up and started walking along the road, heading for Angie's house.

'Quick, we can walk along this side of the road,' John said, as they hurried out the car and walked smartly to shorten the distance between them. As they walked along the D.S. suddenly realised Angie lived along the road. Seemed more than a coincidence, but why would this guy want her dead?

Helen had turned down her radio but kept it loud enough to hear the message coming through that there would be another car there within five minutes.

Colin walked smartly down the street opposite but, apprehensive, turned and checked who was across the road from him.

Helen, without prompting, leaned in and took John's arm playfully, making them look like a happy couple out for a romantic stroll. It was enough to lose Colin's attention for the moment.

Suddenly, a car arrived on the other side of the road, the driver flashing his lights to get Colin's attention before stopping next to him.

Colin got in and turned on the driver angrily.

'What the fuck's going on?'

'The police are on to you,' Terry said.

'Fuck off. You are up to something again.'

'Honest. Angie got a detective to check into her mother's death. He is going to arrest somebody tonight. He said it was a local Kilwinning man. It might not be you, but we can't take the risk, can we? We need to abandon tonight.'

Colin leaned over and grabbed Terry by the shirt front.

'This better be legit. You have been a cunt about this from day one. Honest, man, I could kill you myself the way I feel.'

'For Christ's sake man, I drove all the way back from Edinburgh to warn you. This is the thanks I get.'

Across the street John recognised the car and driver. It was his wife's cousin's husband, Terry. John had always wondered if Angie thought her husband was involved in her mother's death. If she had it looked like she was correct.

'Helen, go back and get the car. I will keep my eye on those two.'

Helen took the car keys and headed the hundred yards back to the police car, hurrying but trying to make it not look obvious.

Terry was on the move again, driving with his new passenger, along and turning into the car park where Colin was parked.

Just them a police car arrived. John waved them down and sent them into the car park and told them not to let the two guys get away. Soon as they could separate them until John and Helen could get there.

The police car immediately put on the blues and two's and swooped into the car park. Helen arrived next to John, and he jumped in, and they sped back to join them in the car park.

John got out and took command. As ordered, the uniforms had Terry out of his car and into theirs while they the plain clothes 2 huckled Colin into their unmarked car.

'What's this all about officer?'

'What's your name, sir?'

'Why?'

'I am asking the questions, sir. Name?'

'Barry Jones.'

'Barry. Barry is it?'

'Yes.'

'Where were you going?'

'Along to my mate, Terry's.'

'And your mate Terry's going to say you are called Barry?'

Colin said nothing but folded his arms, signalling non-compliance.

'What was with the hi-viz then?'

'It's a bit chillier than I expected and it's the only jacket I have with me.'

'So, Barry, why are you driving Colin Allardyce's car?'

Colin hid his face in his hands, Terry had been right all along. They were in the shit. It might not be too bad if Terry could keep his mouth shut.

'I think we need to carry on this conversation back at Saltcoats police station,' John said.

'What? Because I had a hi-viz jacket on going to a mate's house.'

'Then there is the lying to a police officer, not a good start. The position you are in now is that you can volunteer to come to the station with us or we can arrest you. It's up to you?'

'Arrest me for what, wearing a hi-viz jacket in a built-up area after 8 o'clock at night?' he said, trying to make a joke.

'No, it's more like murder.'

That burst his brevity balloon.

Colin folded his arms again, then quietly said, 'okay.'

John got out and left Helen with Colin, instructing her to get his mobile phone and cars keys and anything else from his jacket.

Over at the marked cop car he got in the back of the car beside Terry.

'Hello Terry, fancy seeing you again. Who is your friend in the other car, Terry?'

'Colin. Colin Allardyce. He was going to our house to see us.'

'That's funny, at your mother-in-law's funeral he was Andy Cameron.'

'No, that wasn't Colin, he just looked a bit like him.'

'Funny, because he drove away from the cemetery in Colin's car. Then a moment ago he said he was Barry Jones, yet you say he is Colin.'

John waited until he digested that snippet before going on with the questioning.

'So, why did you stop him down the street and drive him back here?'

Terry thought for a second then said, 'Angie is having one of her heads. She has terrible migraines. She can't abide visitors when she has one of her heads.'

'Terry I would like you to come back to Saltcoats police station so we can carry on this conversation there. Is that okay with you?'

'What for?'

'Well, you already told me a lie, I think if we go to the police station you might decide to start telling the truth. Save us all a lot of time and trouble. You can volunteer to accompany me, or I can arrest you. Obviously I would prefer you to volunteer.'

Terry nodded, 'sure.'

'Right, I need your phone and car keys.'

'What for?'

'So that you can't talk to your friend Colin.'

John pulled an evidence bag from his pocket and Terry dropped his car keys and his mobile in it. 'Anything else in the pockets?'

Terry handed over a few coins and notes.

'Will you bring me back home afterwards?'

John thought for a moment.

'We will see.'

Terry watched as John crossed the car park and got in the police Ford. What had he done? Listening to Colin fucking Allardyce. There again, what had he really done? Spoke to the guy on the train about life and his family. Sure, he had wished his mother-in-law was dead but who didn't diss their family life when they had been drinking.

Shit, the phone. That was the only link. Terry had his in his trouser pocket, John only had his personal phone. If he could get rid of the phone, dump it somewhere in the car on the way and he would be off the hook. Dump it all on Colin. It was all the prick deserved.

THE INTERVIEWS

John and Helen sat in the interview room and prepared the recorder for the first interview with Colin Allardyce.

'Are we doing good cop, bad cop, sir.'

John looked at Helen to see if she was joking. He was sure she hadn't been but when she saw his look she smiled, pretending she had been.

'I talk, you take notes. Okay.'

Helen nodded just as the door opened and Colin Allardyce was shown in by a P.C. He had lost the cockiness he had earlier in the car and looked pale and drawn.

'For the record it is 23:05 on Tuesday the 19th of July. Present are D.S. John Rose, P.C. Helen Begg and Colin Allardyce. At this stage of the interview Mister Allardyce has declined legal representation. Is that correct, Colin.'

Colin nodded.

'For the tape, could you say yes.'

'Yes.'

'Colin, do you know why you are here?'

'No. We were followed into the car park and next thing we were on our way here.'

'Okay, for the record, we are showing photographic evidence, items 1 and 2. Do you recognise the person in these photographs?'

Colin gave them a quick glance then looked away.

'No, could be anybody dressed like that.'

'Could be, but I am confident it is you.'

'No, it's definitely not me.'

'Why did you go to Ina Ralston's funeral?'

'Because Terry Carpenter is my friend.'

'Your friend. Funny, because when I asked Terry at the funeral who you were he said you were Andy Cameron.'

'Must think I am funny.'

'I don't think it's funny. Maybe you don't realise how serious this is. You gave a sample for DNA analysis.'

Colin nodded again.

'Why were you wearing a hi-viz jacket when you were apprehended?'

'I thought it was a bit chilly when I got out of the car. I didn't have another jacket with me, so I just put the hi-viz on.'

John thought and nodded gently as if agreeing with the answer.

'Why wear the hard hat?'

It was Colin's turn to pause.

'Must just have been force of habit, you know, the hat goes with the jacket.'

John picked up one of the photo's again and looked at it without speaking.

They were interrupted then by a knock on the door.

'Interview paused at 23:15 due to outside interruption.'

'Come,' John called out, and the door opened slightly. He was summoned outside by the P.C. who had shown Colin in.

'Just be a minute.'

Outside the door the uniform showed John a mobile phone in an evidence bag.

'Where was that?'

'Pushed down the back seat of the car you were using.'

'Oh, right. Obviously Mister Allardyce was naïve enough to think it was that easy to get rid of. Thanks Eric.'

John went back into the interview room and sat the phone down on the table but didn't acknowledge anything about it.

'Interview restarted at 23:18. Same people present.'

John noticed Colin looked away from the table and the phone and photographs that lay on it.

'As I was saying before we were interrupted, you volunteered a DNA sample. We retrieved an unknown DNA sample from Ina Ralston's house. I have reason to believe it will turn out to be your DNA. If it is, could you be able to explain how your DNA got there?'

'It won't be mine; I have never been in the woman's house. I don't even know where she lived.'

John picked up the plastic pouch with the mobile phone in it and examined it through the polythene.

'What can you tell me about this phone?'

Colin looked at it with a puzzled look on his face.

'Never seen it before.'

'So, you don't know where we found it?'

'No. Why would I?'

'Helen, it's not yours is it?'

'No, sir. Never seen it before.'

'Well, it was found pushed down the back seat of the Focus. It will be checked for fingerprints later today. Plus, the techs here will know who used it and who they were calling.'

'Even if it was mine, what does it prove?'

'Do you ever do jigsaws, Colin?'

'No, not for years.'

'You see I think investigation is like a jigsaw. I am collecting all the parts at the moment and bit by bit they will come together and eventually I will have the full picture.'

Colin smiled, what kind of cop was this, he thought? Modern day investigating, doing jigsaws, he shook his head.

'So, what is your relationship with Terry Carpenter?'

'Just a guy I know. I met him on the train home from Glasgow and we got on well. We were talking about going out one night together with our wives and we had arranged for me to meet her that night.'

'Arranged for you to meet her, just you? Why not bring your wife along?'

'Look, we were drunk when we arranged it. You know what it's like?'

'No, I don't really.'

'Oh, is that another piece of the jigsaw?'

'Most of our evidence is circumstantial at the moment but there will be traces of your DNA or fingerprints out there.'

Colin laughed, regaining a bit of his cockiness now that he thought the detective was a bit defective.

'This is unbelievable, just because the old woman went to bed with her teeth in.'

He realised he had just about admitted guilt when he looked up and saw the reaction from the D.S. and the P.C. who turned to look at each other, their expressions similar as if they had just watched their 6th ball drop from the Lotto machine.

'Well, Mister Allardyce, if you have nothing more to say I suggest we terminate this interview, the time is now 23:47.'

John stopped the tape then got up to open the interview room door.

'I want a lawyer,' Colin said, suddenly serious.

'Certainly, sir. Eric will see you have representation for our next interview.'

When he left and the door closed, John punched the air.

'What a plonker, practically admitting guilt. After all, apart from a few people, who would know the crux of the case started with Ina Ralston keeping her teeth in.'

'Bet you when he comes back in his lawyer will have him button up and no comment everything.'

'Well, I am confident we will get something from his DNA. Right, coffee then we bring Carpenter in. See what he has to say.'

Before they started Terry Carpenter's interview John and Helen received news from the Troon plods that had transferred Terry over from the car park to Saltcoats. They had found a mobile phone beneath the driver's seat. The description made it sound similar to Colin's hidden phone.

Somebody was bringing it over.

'Are we waiting for the phone?' Helen asked her boss.

'No, that will be a wee surprise for him, same as Colin got.'

There was a knock on the door and Terry walked in.

'Take a seat.'

Terry looked dishevelled and tired.

'Interview on 20th July at 00:45 hrs, present are Detective Sergeant John Rose, Police Constable Helen Begg and Terry Carpenter. Before the interview Mister Carpenter refused legal representation. For the benefit of the tape Terry could you say you agree with this.'

'Yes, I agree.'

'Right, Terry, we are currently carrying out an investigation into what we are calling the Tuesday night killers.'

Terry looked puzzled.

'Over the past 18 months or so there have been a number of deaths on a Tuesday night in Kilwinning which were put down to Covid, but many were unexplained. Your mother-in-law's was one of those.'

John turned the photograph's over.

'For the record, I am showing Mister Carpenter exhibits 1 and 2. Do you recognise the man in these pictures?'

Terry looked as if he was trying hard to recognise the guy in the hi-viz.

He shrugged, 'sorry, he could be anybody.'

'We think it is your friend Colin Allardyce.'

'Well, he isn't really my friend. I met him on the train home from a night out and I agreed to look at his pension. I am a pension consultant, and I went to his house to discuss his pension.'

'Why did you pick him up tonight?'

Terry's head dropped.

'It's embarrassing because your wife is my wife's cousin, but I have to admit I ended up having a bit of a fling with Colin's wife and he was going to my house to tell all to my wife.'

John looked at Helen before continuing.

'Bit of a fling?' John echoed his words.

He shrugged again, as if it wasn't a big thing. 'We had sex a couple of times?'

'Both on the same night?' Helen interjected.

'What's that got to do with it?' Terry said, bemused.

'We are just trying to establish if it was a one off occasion or if you met up on more occasions.'

Terry thought about it.

'We met twice.'

There was a silence then John restarted the questions.

'Why was Colin wearing hi-viz gear and a hard hat?'

'You will need to ask him.'

'Oh, we have. Said he was cold, but it certainly wasn't cold last night, it was still hot at 9 o'clock.'

John picked one of the photographs and looked at it, again without speaking for a minute.

'I thought there definitely was a likeness when I saw him walking towards your house tonight.'

They were interrupted by another knock at the door.

John got up this time and reached out and took the phone he was expecting, from the P.C.

'For the benefit of the record, I am showing Terry exhibit 4. Do you recognise this?'

Terry shrugged.

'It's a mobile phone.'

'Yes, it's the mobile phone you put beneath the driver's seat of the squad car.'

'Not me, never seen that before.'

'Yes, I am afraid it is yours. All police cars are checked before they go on duty and are checked again when somebody is arrested. It's amazing the things people absent-mindedly leave behind.'

Terry continued to shake his head.

'Amazingly, Colin left a phone the exact same make and model in our car. That's more than a coincidence.'

John held up both evidence bags with identical phones in them. 'I am showing Terry exhibit 3, the identical phone belonging to Colin Allardyce and exhibit 4, the phone found in the car he was brought to the station tonight. Hard to tell the difference.

Just because you have locked them doesn't mean we can't find out who has been using them and when you called each other.'

The D.S. waited in case Terry had anything to add. Then he picked the picture of the hi-viz man again.

'So, back to the hi-viz, if you look at the picture again, you will have to admit there is a similarity between Colin and the guy in the picture.'

'I don't think so. If I wore hi-viz and a hard hat I might look like the guy in the picture.'

'Have you discussed your mother-in-law with Colin?'

'We spoke about our families so she must have come up in the conversation at some time.'

'Did you speak about her passing?'

'No, I don't think so.'

'What did you speak about in the cemetery at the funeral? It seemed pretty heated.'

'What? No, he was just apologising for not sending us a wee sympathy card.'

'Not much to get heated about. Well, Terry, as I said earlier, this is a major investigation. We are talking dozens of murders, there must have been more than one person planning and doing all this.'

Before Terry had a chance to say anything, John stopped the interview.

'Right, let's wrap it up there. Interview terminated at 01:26 hours.'

John got up and opened the door for Terry to go out.

'What did Angie say when you said you had been arrested?'

Terry looked him straight in the eye.

'I haven't told her.'

'Did you use your phone call?'

'Yes,' he said, then left to go back to his cell.

Helen was picking the evidence bags off the table when John turned to her.

'Can you believe that, he used his phone call and didn't tell his wife. Probably phoned his fancy bit, if that was true.'

Helen looked up without speaking.

'By the way, you wrong footed him with the question about the number of times he met up with Sadie. He was lying. Not that he told us the truth that much.'

'It was just the way he said a couple of times.'

'Right, our plan is to go home, grab a couple of hours sleep and come back about 9 a.m. How does that sound to you? That gives us a chance to get some results from forensics, but I know there still won't be. It will give Terry and Colin a long time to think about the trouble they are actually in.'

'Right, sir. Back for 9 then.'

John drove out of the secure parking area at the police station and immediately phoned Angie. It rang and rang and rang. He kept expecting it to go to her answering machine, but it didn't, it just kept ringing.

A few minutes later his car phone rang, it was Angie.

'Hello, did you call me?' she said, still sounding sleepy.

'Angie, it's John Rose. I have some bad news for you, your husband has been arrested.'

There was a long silence on the line. John was about to repeat the message when Angie finally spoke.

'When you said it was bad news I thought he was dead. Hold on, he is at a course in Edinburgh. Did they phone you from there and ask you to tell me?'

'No, he was arrested in Troon.'

'Troon. Hold on, is this for real or am I dreaming.'

'No. At this moment this is off the record really, I am phoning as a friend.'

'So, what has he done, can you tell me that.'

'When I told you we were going to arrest the person who we thought had killed your mother tonight, well, we did. At the time of his arrest, he was in the company of your husband, and he was arrested too. At the moment he is helping us with our enquiries.'

'What are you saying?'

'I have said all I can. I think you can work it out for yourself. I can also say he was arrested and brought into custody at 9 o'clock last night so by 9 o'clock tonight he will either be arrested or allowed to go free.'

'What is this all about?'

'Angie, I have told you all I can at the moment. As soon as there are any developments you will be the first to know.'

'Right, thanks John, bye.'

'Bye.'

John arrived back at the incident room just before 9 o'clock as arranged. Helen was already there and standing at the whiteboard.

She had obviously showered before leaving home, John could smell the freshness off her. He had showered too but it wasn't obvious on him.

'What are you thinking?'

'In this case, I think we could have the why. If Terry wanted his mother-in-law dead he must have got Colin to do it?'

'That might be the case, but we still don't know why, or if he did, what he offered in return?'

'What if it was something to do with this affair he was having with Colin's wife?'

'Helen, I think we have our next step. Come on, let's go to Kilwinning and speak to Colin's wife.'

Helen drove, as usual, and they were making good time until they got stuck at road works on the main road through Kilwinning.

'What do you think Colin's wife, Sadie, is like? Do you think she will be a poser like him?'

'Who knows? You know the saying, opposites attract, she might be like him, she might be a plain jane.'

'What's your wife like? Like you or the opposite?'

'Christ, no, she couldn't be like me. I would do my nut in if she was the same as me. We would have split up or one of us would have killed the other if we were. What about you? Is there anybody in your life?'

John had learned from his mistakes, nowadays you couldn't assume a woman has a male friend, he was treading carefully.

'No, nobody. It's hard to start a relationship when you are on these shifts.'

'Yes, I suppose you are right.'

'How are we going to tackle Sadie Allardyce?'

'We will just try and let her do the talking. Women like to talk.'

'So do some men,' she said brusquely.

'Touché,' John said with a wry smile.

Sadie opened the door, still in her pyjamas, no doubt from being disturbed the night before.

John showed his identity card and introduced himself and his assistant.

'Do you mind if we come in and ask you a few questions?'

Sadie never replied but walked through to the lounge and allowed them to follow.

Sadie sat in her chair and motioned for the coppers to sit on the sofa.

'You will know why we are here; your husband being arrested last night.'

'Has he been charged?'

'No. At the moment he is helping us with our enquiries into a number of deaths in Kilwinning and possibly surrounding areas.'

'A number?'

'Over the past 18 months there have been an abnormally high numbers of deaths in the town and more so on a Tuesday night. Did your husband go out on a Tuesday night?'

Sadie was stunned. She thought she was going to be interviewed about her husband's involvement in new lover's mother-in-law's death, not about a lot more deaths.

Straight away she thought it was a chance to drop her husband in it, whether he was some crazed serial killer or not, she now had the chance to push him along the guilty route.

What she didn't know was, if he was some serial killer, was he doing it on his own or was her Terry an assistant in all that.

'Mrs. Allardyce, did you hear the question?'

'What? He was out every Tuesday night, allegedly drinking with workmates but I suspected he had a lover. Maybe I was wrong on that score.'

John and Helen glimpsed over at each other, encouragingly.

'So, on an average Tuesday night he would be out until what time?'

'He would never be back before after 10:30. Normally I would be asleep when he came in, so it could have been even later.'

'Did you ever see any blood on his clothes?'

'No, not blood. I used to examine his boxers but when I started to find dried in, you know stuff, and I knew he was up to something I stopped looking at his clothes, just threw them in the wash.'

'Colin was arrested along with Terry Carpenter. Do you know him?'

Again, Sadie waited before answering.

'Terry came here to check over Colin's pension paperwork. He is a pension consultant.'

'Nothing else, he seemed to indicate he knew better than that?' Helen said, speaking for the first time.

'We were lovers,' she said quietly, then looked down at her wedding band.

John and Helen kept deadpan, not letting their interviewee know if she was saying the right thing for her lover or not. They also kept quiet for a moment to see if she added to her admission.

'How long have you been lovers for?' Helen followed up by asking.

'Only 2 or 3 weeks.'

'How long have you known him?' asked John, taking his turn again.

'Only 2 or 3 weeks.'

'Did you know his mother-in-law died recently?'

'Yes, I think he did mention it.'

'You didn't go to her funeral?'

'No. I didn't know her.'

'Did Colin go to her funeral?'

'No, why would he?'

'No reason, just things we have to get clear.'

John turned round to Helen. 'That's all I have to ask. Helen, have you anything else?'

'On a Tuesday, did he always wear the same clothes?'

'How do you mean?'

'Well, you said you thought he went to his girlfriends every Tuesday. Was he particular about what he wore?'

'He has 2 suits. He wears the black one Monday and Tuesday, Wednesday and Thursday he wears his dark blue one then back to the black one on a Friday.'

'Does he get it cleaned in-between.'

'No. He might seem to be suave man about town but deep down he is a miserable sod. He would only get his suit cleaned if it was visibly dirty.'

They stood up to go when John turned round to Sadie again.

'Sadie, did you know, or suspect Colin had killed or had any part in the death of anybody?'

'No,' she said. Then added, 'if I had I would have told you myself.'

'Right, thanks for your time. If you think of anything else, here's my card.'

Sadie took it without even looking at it.

Helen started the car's engine and they pulled away from the Allardyce residence.

'Well, what do you think?' John asked.

'She was pausing, not wanting to drop anyone in it.'

'Yes, that's what I thought too. Anything else?'

'Yes, she paused when you asked her at the end. She knows something.'

'What would you do, take her in for more questioning?'

'No, not just now. She will be sweating over this all day. I would wait until after we decide to charge the men in her life or not.'

'Do you know, that's exactly what I was thinking.'

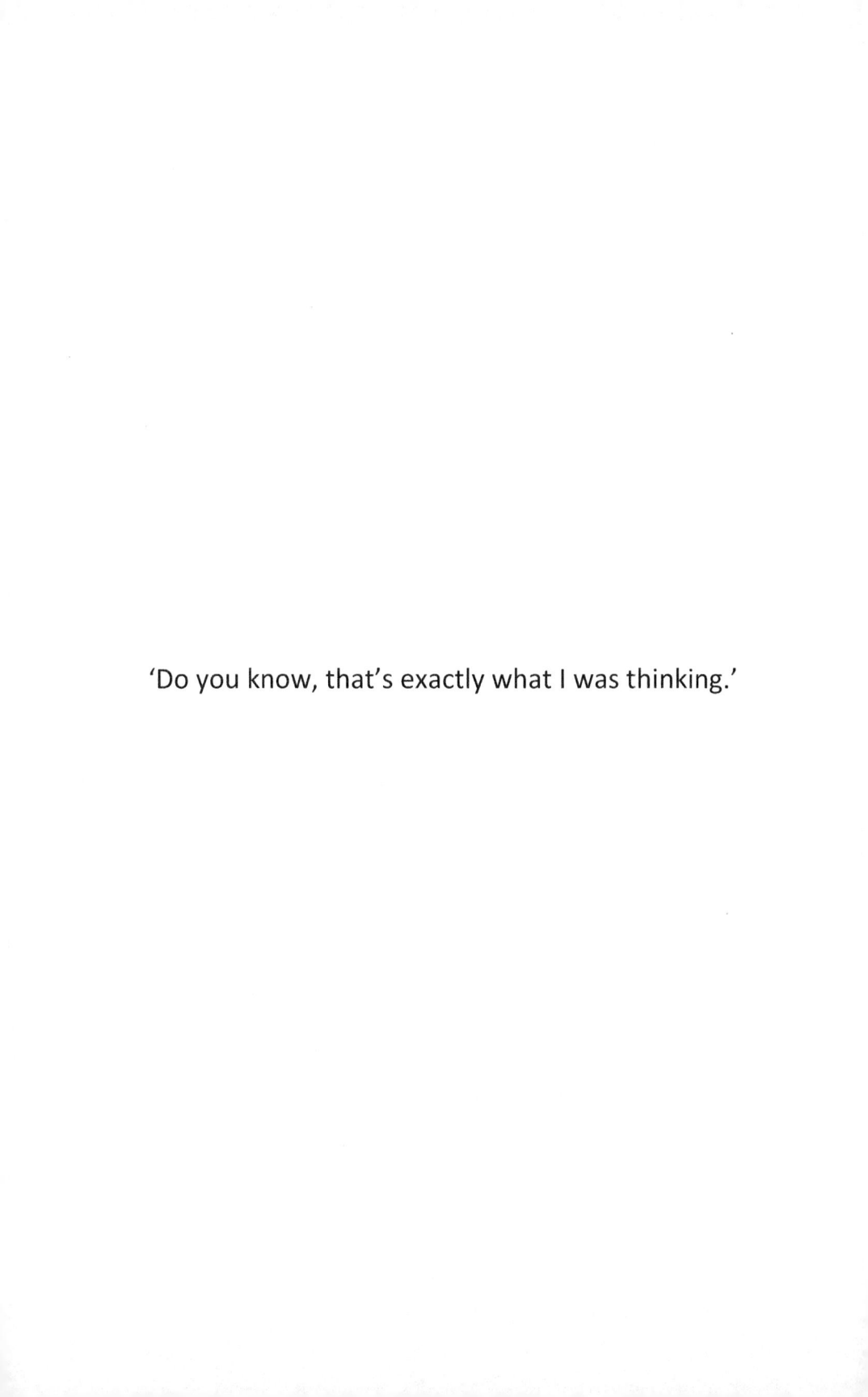

THE SECOND INTERVIEW, COLIN

'Interview on 20th July 2022 at 10:15 hrs, present are Detective Sergeant John Rose, Police Constable Helen Begg, Colin Allardyce and his solicitor, Robin Nelson.'

'Mister Allardyce, do you work for Scottish Water?'

'No.'

'Have you ever worked for Scottish Water?'

'No.'

Robin Nelson was scribbling away at his large yellow pad and glimpsing over at his client as he did so.

John Rose took an evidence bag from his pocket.

'For the benefit of the record, I am showing Mister Allardyce a false identity card supposedly saying Mister Allardyce works for Scottish Water.

How would you explain this?' he asked as he showed the bag, inside it was the fake i.d. he had made up to show to Ina Ralston and had planned to use again with her daughter Angie.

Robin Nelson put a hand up.

'Detective Rose, may I remind you it is up to you to put your case to us, not for us to explain things to you.'

John expected this when he heard who Colin's brief was. Nelson was the kind of guy who you would want to defend you but an absolute prick when you were against him.

John smiled sardonically.

'Mister Allardyce, this obviously fake identity badge was found in the pocket of your hi-viz jacket you were wearing when you came into the police station. Can you explain what it is?'

'Once again you are asking my client to explain,' Nelson interjected again.

John Rose put his hand up to stop him.

'Mister Allardyce, I believe you used this fake identity to gain entry to Ina Ralston's house where you subsequently murdered her. I also believe you were heading to Angie Carpenter's house to do the same.'

'No comment,' Colin said quietly.

'For the benefit of the tape could you please speak a bit louder and clearer.'

'No comment,' he said, increasing his voice several notches.

The D.S. then lifted another evidence bag, this time it contained a quantity of blue nitrile gloves.

'For the benefit of the tape I am showing evidence bag 6 which contains a selection of blue nitrile disposable gloves.

These nitrile gloves were also found in the hi-viz jacket you were wearing when apprehended last night. If you look again at the 2nd picture I showed you last night, the man in the hi-viz jacket is wearing similar gloves. Is this you Colin?'

'No, it's not me. Okay, I had the identity card made up for a fancy-dress party I was going to,' Colin said, trying to sound light-hearted. As he spoke he glimpsed at his brief who was wanting him to shut up.

'Where was this party?'

Realising he shouldn't have said anything before he simply answered, 'no comment.'

'Colin, I don't think you realise how much trouble you are in. This old woman's murder is just the tip of the iceberg. My team are looking into around 60 other cases of unexplained deaths that we have found in the 18 months or so since Covid hit Scotland.'

Colin went very quiet for a moment, then added, again in a quiet voice, that he wanted time to speak to his lawyer.

'Interview paused at 10:53 to allow Mister Allardyce to speak to his lawyer.'

John Rose watched the accused and brief walk out. When the door closed behind them he turned to Helen with a huge grin on his face.

'We've got him?'

'Are you sure?'

'I've done enough of these cases to know when somebody knows the game is up. Last night Allardyce was all bravado, thinking he was smarter than us. My next move was to say we had interviewed his wife and she couldn't provide him with an alibi for any Tuesday nights. I didn't even need to get that far.'

'So, what will he admit to?'

'Pretty sure it will just be the Ralston woman. Pound to a penny he throws Carpenter under the bus with him.'

'What do we do now?'

'Time for a coffee, I think. They will be back within the hour.'

'Interview commenced 12:10, present are Detective Sergeant John Rose, Police Constable Helen Begg, Colin Allardyce and his legal representative Robin Nelson.'

Robin Nelson stood up and lifted a prepared statement ready to read it out.

John Rose could tell from his body language he wasn't happy. To an up and coming and highly regarded attorney admitting guilt at such an early stage of the interview process was like admitting defeat on his part.

'Mister Colin Allardyce would like to put on the record he was at the home of Ina Ralston on the night in question. This statement is in his words.

I met Terry Carpenter on a train, returning from a night out in Glasgow. I had partaken a lot of alcoholic drink that evening and somewhat foolishly agreed to help his mother-in-law to Heaven, as Mister Carpenter put it to me.

I admit I went to meet the woman that night but had no intention to murder her, just to see if she was as old and infirm she as he had told me she was.

After gaining access to the home the old lady clasped her chest and fell at my feet. I panicked and put her in her bed with the intention of phoning an ambulance from a phone box. When I got back to my car I drove round the town looking for a phone box but there are none in operation now, so I just went home. I realise now I should have alerted the emergency services but that is my only crime.

I have nothing to do with any other suspicious deaths and will only answer no comment to any further questions.'

Robin sat down next to his client, who had been sitting with his head down since re-entering the interview room.

'There are still a lot of questions to be answered, a lot of loose ends to be tied up. What did Terry Carpenter agree to do for you?'

'No comment,' Colin answered the Detective.

'How much did your wife know about Ina Ralston's death?'

'No comment.'

'What did you do in the bathroom sink?'

'No comment.'

John turned to Helen.

'Is there anything you want to ask he won't answer?'

Helen shook her head slightly having sensed defeat.

'If you have nothing to add, interview terminated at 12:25.'

There was a screeching of chairs as Colin Allardyce and his lawyer made a quick exit. When the door closed behind them the two police turned to each other and smiled.

'Knew we had him.'

'But he is only admitting to the one killing. Not exactly admitting it but surely a jury wouldn't believe him, that she just died.'

'He might actually be telling the truth. it might be the only he did, but now we have his DNA if he did anything else, he has no place to hide.'

'You know this is quite amazing, all because that woman said about her mother still having her teeth on in bed. Do you think there is any chance she she did take just have a heart attack?'

'Heart attack my arse. He has had 14 hours to come up with something, suppose he has done okay, but we could possibly still exhume the body. Wouldn't be right, really.

Next, I think it's time we brought Sadie Allardyce to the station, and we will have another go at Terry Carpenter. After lunch, of course.'

AN INSPECTOR CALLS

Before they could go to lunch, there was a knock on the interview room door. Paul Lindsay, the desk sergeant, popped his head in.

'Walker wants to see you.'

'Both of you, and now,' he added.

'Sounds ominous,' Helen said.

'Probably just wanting an update,' her superior said but not believing it.

The Detective Inspector's office door was open, an unusual occurrence, normally he thrived on having his privacy.

'Sit!' he ordered.

'Well, team, how is it going?'

'Allardyce had admitted he was in Ina Ralston's house but claims she had a heart attack and died on the spot.'

'Good. Very good. Which of you went to the local press?'

The two coppers looked at each other, bemused.

'The press? Not us,' D.S. Rose said without even consulting his assistant.

The Inspector turned his computer screen that was open at the local newspaper, the North Ayrshire Advertiser. The headline, Kilwinning Serial Killer?

'The facts stated are almost exactly what you put on the initial report to me. How do you explain that?'

'Who else saw the report?' John asked.

'Who else, who fucking else? Nobody else from my desk!' he said, his nostrils flaring in anger.

'I can categorically assure you it didn't come from any of us,' the D.S. said confidently.

The 2 men turned and looked at Helen.

'Not me. Why would I, I've loved working this case, why would I jeopardise it?'

'Look sir, we have put a lot of work into this case. Why would we go to the press when we were on the verge of getting a result?'

'Maybe it was because I threatened to put you off the case!' the D.I. said, raising his voice again.

'If it turns out it came from one of us I will resign.'

'Well, that would be a bonus. Now I will need to deny it but I will need to put more bodies on the case. Bodies I am struggling to afford, there is a series of big drugs bust in the pipeline and officers are needed for that.'

The D.I. sighed then continued.

'I will tell you something, if there are any more details leaked to the press then you two are off the case. Okay, now get out!'

In the corridor Helen whispered to her boss. 'I need a word.'

John looked over at her without speaking, he hoped she wasn't going to confess to him, he would not be happy after speaking up for her and putting his job on the line.

They went back into the interview room where they could talk in privacy.

'Well,' John said, crossing his arms as he waited for her to talk.

'I think it might be my fault.'

'Your,' he said before Helen silenced him by raising a hand at him.

'I was defending you in the canteen. The other P.C.s were slagging you off and I threw a few statistics at them, proving you were onto something in the case.'

'Who do you think spilled the beans then?'

'Honestly, I don't know sir. It will be public knowledge already and nobody will grass their mates.'

'Right, we better get something to eat and get the other one singing like a canary.'

INTERVIEW TWO, TERRY

Since the last interview, Terry had also lawyered up. Colin's brief was up and coming, Terry's was more down and out. Henry Muir was well past retirement age and walked with a definite stoop. He had a look of Mister Burns from the Simpson's about him.

They settled into the interview room and Helen worked the recorder and introduced the attendees.

'Interview commencing at 14:15 hours. Present are Detective Sergeant John Rose, Police Constable Helen Begg, Terry Carpenter and his lawyer Henry Muir.'

Henry started by putting his hand up slightly, indicating he wanted to intervene.

'Point of order, D.S. Rose. I feel an interview of this importance should only be carried out by two detectives.'

John knew the old duffer would want to get away on the right foot, get brownie points, but he picked the wrong argument to start with.

'A case like what?'

Henry's mouth opened and shut like a fish, an involuntary action he had, as he tried to think of his counter argument.

'Well, well,' he blustered, 'according to my client you seem to be implicating in some airy-fairy idea he is implicated in series of murder plots.'

'So, why does that affect who is assisting me? I don't know if you noticed that over the last 18 month or so we had a pandemic. The roles within Scottish police have had to adjust to the new norm.

Unless you think a woman cannot do the job of a man.'

More fish faces before Henry said, 'just carry on then.'

John took a breath before continuing. He only wished now he had asked Helen to lead the questioning, that would have had the old crank's gander right up.

'Mister Carpenter, we now have a statement from Colin Allardyce regarding the death of your mother-in-law, Ina Ralston. Would you now furnish us with your version of the events?'

Terry glanced at his lawyer who shook his head gently before saying, 'no comment.'

'Gentlemen, we both know only the guilty hide behind the no comment strategy. The fact that your co-conspirator has told us his part doesn't mean we know the truth but only his version of it.

We are still waiting on DNA results and that could implicate you and him even further.'

Terry and his lawyer started whispering.

'For the benefit of the tape Mister Carpenter and his lawyer are conferring,' Helen said, as there would be inaudible mumbling on the recording.

'Perhaps it better if you ask the questions and my client will furnish the answers as far as he can.'

'Thank you Henry. Terry, how do you know Colin Allardyce?'

'I already told you, we met on the train home from a night out. Well, separate nights out, I didn't know him until we sat together on the train.'

'It was then you discussed him killing your mother-in-law, was it?'

'No, that wasn't how it came about. We were just sort of bellyaching about how life would be better if things were different.'

John kept quiet, hoping Terry would keep talking to fill the void.

'I just said if my mother-in-law wasn't alive then my wife and I could move to Portugal.'

'What did he say was wrong with his life?'

Terry thought before speaking again. 'Oh, he was worried about his financial situation. He had a lover who he wanted to leave his wife for. As I am a pensions adviser I offered to check out his financial situation with regard to his pensions.'

'He agreed to kill your mother-in-law in return for you looking at his pensions. You have had 15 hours or so and that's the best you have come up with.'

'It's true.'

'So, what about the mobile phones yourself and Mister Allardyce tried to hide in the police cars.'

'No comment.'

'Although they may be locked, it will take our techs just minutes to find out who you have been calling and when. They are doing that just now, I am expecting the results shortly.'

'No comment.'

John Rose then held up another evidence bag.

'For the benefit of the tape I am showing Mister Carpenter pieces of paper with names and addresses on them.

So, Terry, these pieces of paper were found in Colin Allardyce's hi-viz jacket pocket. I don't need to tell you, do I, that the names and addresses are your mother-in-law and your wife's. I believe this is your writing.'

John had matched them to his writing when he was signed into the police station.

Terry looked raging for a second but then tried to shrug it off.

'No comment.'

Terry then raised a hand and leaned into speak to his brief again.

'For the record Mister Carpenter and his lawyer are conferring,' Helen said.

After the chinwag Henry Muir stood up.

'Lady, gentleman, my client and I would like to carry on our consultation in private.'

Terry stood up beside him and they left the interview room.

'Interview terminated at 14:37 hrs.'

The door closed and the Detective Sergeant turned and smiled again.

'We've got him.'

'Are you sure?'

'Yes. It was when I showed him the pieces of paper. I think he told Colin to destroy them but obviously he kept them. We just need to wait now. Celebratory coffee?'

'Sure, I need something strong inside me,' Helen said smiling, as she put her hand on top of his.

John looked at her to see if she was laughing or giving a genuine come-on. The smile on her face said it was the latter. All through the investigation, well after the first few days, he had managed to compartmentalise their relationship to strictly business. Maybe the line between business and pleasure was dissolving.

John put his other hand on top of hers.

'Coffee first.'

TWO NIL

John and Helen had finished their coffees and were in the incident room. They only had a corner now as the drugs team had commandeered the majority of the room.

While Helen continued writing up the extensive reports from the interviews John paced in front of their white board.

'What's wrong, not so confident now?' Helen asked. The movement annoying her.

'No, it's the procurator. I just hope she accepts a murder charge for Allardyce with what we have. I am sure the DNA will sink him but that won't come through before tonight.'

'Who is the fiscal? We just email our reports into the department, I have never had a direct dealing with him.'

'Her. Amanda Murdoch. I have never dealt with her, since she was appointed I have been up in the cupboard.'

They hadn't noticed the office door opening or the Inspector approach and overhear their conversation.

'Amanda Murdoch is very astute. If the case is strong enough she will hit it hard. So, what have you got?'

'Allardyce has confessed to being in the Ralston woman's house but says she conveniently dropped dead. Carpenter is on the verge of confessing but, as yet we don't know what he will own up to.'

'What about the serial killer angle?'

'Too early to say but my gut is that this is a one-off.'

'So what, there is no serial killer?'

'Too early to tell.'

There was a knock on the incident room door. The desk sergeant stood just inside the room.

'Sadie Allardyce is downstairs, and Terry Carpenter and his lawyer want a word, sir.'

'Thanks, Paul. Duty calls, sir.'

'Right, keep me in the loop,' Walker said, before striding away.

'Well, Helen, who first?'

'Sadie. Might let something slip we can use with Terry.'

'Sadie it is then.'

'Interview with Sadie Allardyce, also present are Detective Sergeant John Rose and P.C. Helen Begg.'

Helen was again in charge of the recorder; John started the questioning.

'Do you prefer Mrs. Allardyce or Sadie?' he asked, trying to relax her.

She looked like a rabbit caught in the headlights. She imagined being questioned in an office somewhere, in an interview room was something different.

'Sadie, you are here of your own volition. However, if you aren't willing to talk we may have to arrest you. Do you understand?'

'Yes,' she said meekly.

'You said your husband went out every Tuesday night and didn't return until after 10:30, is that correct?'

'Yes.'

'He introduced you to Terry Carpenter. How did he know him?'

'He said somebody in the office had used his services and he was very good.'

'You said you have only known him for about 3 weeks and have been lovers since then. Did you know he was a married man?'

'Yes. He told me he wasn't happy with her because.' Then she stopped before continuing, 'he wasn't happy with her.'

'Because?'

She thought for a moment.

'Because she didn't want to go and live abroad with him.'

'She must be crazy, I would love to live abroad,' Helen said, joining in with the conversation hoping to draw something else from her. After she spoke she hoped John wouldn't be angry with her.

'I know,' Sadie said, 'I offered to go with him.'

They all smiled, as if it was a throwaway comment but the two police thought differently. Helen's comment had worked.

'Did Terry ask your husband to kill his mother-in-law?'

Sadie looked down at her hands that were in her lap at the time.

'No.'

'Colin has already told us he went to her house.'

There was a shocked look on her face.

'I never knew,' she said, looking back in her lap again.

'You were having sex with Terry and didn't know he ordered his mother-in-law's death.'

The question was rhetorical, and John changed the tact.

'Why was your husband going to Terry's house last night?'

She continued looking at her hands.

'I don't know.'

'He had already killed Terry's mother-in-law, was he going to kill his wife so that you two could sail off into the sunset?'

John was out on a limb, guessing what might have been going on. He was certain Colin was going there probably with malice aforethought. Sadie's reaction practically confirmed it.

Sadie's head shot up from where she had been looking and stared straight at John.

'Who told you that?'

'I cannot say, but you are not denying it, are you?'

'I didn't know he was going there. We don't talk, he tells me nothing.'

'If you were involved in any planning you will be getting charged as well.'

'Anything they did didn't involve me.'

John reckoned he wouldn't get anything more from her so turned to Helen.

'Anything you want to ask?'

'What did your husband think about your relationship with Terry?'

'He wasn't bothered. I told you, he has a lover.'

'Thank you Sadie,' John said, then Helen concluded the interview.

'Right, Sadie, we will arrange your lift home.'

'What happens next?'

'With who?'

'Terry. My husband never even told me he had been arrested.'

'All the evidence will be passed to the procurator fiscal who will decide if there are to be charged. We will know by 9 o'clock tonight, one way or another.'

Terry Carpenter and his solicitor took their places in the interview room and Helen started the recorder. Henry Muir stood up and read a statement.

'My client, Terry Carpenter, admits he discussed with Colin Allardyce killing his mother-in-law Ina Ralston. He knew she had cancer and thought it was an act of mercy.

He also admits having an affair with Sadie Allardyce and found out Colin was going to tell his wife about the affair last night which was why he met him last night and intercepted him before he could speak to her.

At this time, he wishes not to answer any more questions. If you do ask anything he will simply answer no comment.'

Henry then sat down again.

'If that's it we will terminate the interview.'

Helen ended the recording and Carpenter and Muir promptly left.

'Right, Helen, let's get all this stuff written up and off to the proc.'

WAITING, WAITING, WAITING

John and Helen went for a pre-celebration dinner. As they drove to the local Chinese restaurant John had insisted they both had steaks. Big thick juicy sirloins which he preferred a bit pink inside.

It was only when Helen parked up that she told him that she was a vegetarian. He was really surprised; she was the first vegan or veggie who hadn't told him within 5 minutes of being introduced that eating meat was appalling.

Instead of going full beef, John opted for a beef curry. Helen opted for a veggie one.

'Have you ever tried vegetable curry?' Helen asked.

The very thought of a meal without some form of meat was completely alien to John.

'No, never.'

'Want a try?'

No, he thought, but he wanted back on his partner's good books.

'Sure.'

Helen put a bit of some kind of spicy veg on her fork and offered it across the table.

John leaned across and took it in his mouth. Sitting back, he chewed it then swallowed, his eyes opening in amazement at the taste.

'Wow, did you like it?'

Like it, he hated it. However, the Oscar for the best performance of a confirmed meat eater pretending to like vegetarian curry went to John Rose.

'Loved it, I will need to try it one night.'

Helen smiled as she thought she had a new convert.

After their food they went back to the station to wait. Their case notes were sent earlier to the procurator fiscal. They were very hopeful of charges but there were no certainties once it was out of their hands.

They were alone in the incident room again, the rest of the detectives off on their planned drugs raid.

'What are the alternatives?' Helen asked. She obviously knew the process from her police college work, but this was real, this wasn't theory.

'As far as Colin Allardyce goes, there are options. Best result is one charge of murder and one of attempted murder. The second murder charge is a bit woolly but the other thing is if you throw more at him he might plead guilty to lesser charges. In his case, I think the Ina Ralston murder is a stick-on.'

'What about Carpenter?'

'Ideally we would get two cases of conspiracy to murder. It's the same with him. The first case of his mother-in-law should be a definite but the second, his wife, is more of a hunch. Of course, there is always the third decision, to keep them in custody for another 24 hours to gain more evidence.'

'Would that help?'

'Not really. We won't get anything from forensics in another day and they have already confessed in part. Realistically, they are unlikely to say anything else.'

While they waited Helen continued to work at her computer, looking for any other evidence that might help later in the case. John meantime, busied himself at the whiteboard, marking down what information he had, what evidence they had and lastly what his theories were that still had to be proven, one way or another.

On cue almost, at 20:45 Inspector Walker walked into the incident room. John thought he didn't look so happy, although that was nothing new.

The two cops stopped what they were doing and gave their boss their full attention, hoping for good news.

'John, when you came to me with your proposal for this case I have to admit I thought it was whimsical, to say the least. Even though Helen delivered a great report I was still sceptical, I mean, a serial killer in Kilwinning?'

John felt like walking over and grabbing the pompous, arrogant twat by the throat. Get to the point, he thought.

'Anyway, Amanda Murdoch gave your reports and has agreed we proceed with all 4 charges. Well done.'

John turned to Helen who was smiling, confirming he had heard correctly, all 4 charges.

'Right, let's get them charged,' the Inspector said as he turned and left them.

Although not p.c., John crossed over and hugged Helen.

'What a team,' he said.

As they separated, Helen took his arm.

'John, I want to thank you for everything you have taught me. I learned more about police work in the short time we have been together than all the time at the college or on the beat.'

'Thanks. Not bad for an old dinosaur. Right, we better get them charged. I will need to call the wife, tell her I should be home about half past 9.'

Helen took his hand. 'Why not say you will be a bit later, we could go to my place and celebrate.'

'I can't drink and drive.'

'I didn't say drink, just celebrate.'

HE'S BEEN CHARGED

After the two guys were charged, John and Helen nipped back to the incident room to call the two wives. Helen phoned Sadie while John called Angie.

Angie answered the call almost immediately, obviously waiting on the call.

'Angie, it's John. Terry has just been charged with 2 counts of conspiracy to murder.'

He heard her draw a breath.

'He really was involved in my mother's death.'

'I am sorry to have to tell you but yes, it seems so.'

'Who was the other person?'

'You.'

'Me, really? No way.'

'It seems so. He wanted you out of the picture so he could hitch up with his lover.'

'No, you are wrong there. Terry has a lover, Terry! Are you sure?'

'Did you not think it funny that he didn't contact you last night and tell you he had been charged? He phoned her.'

'I, well, you,' she rambled, as she tried to make sense of what she was hearing.

'I just thought he used the call to contact his lawyer.'

'No, we would do that for him.'

'Oh, God, I can't believe this.'

'Right, tell you what, I will come over tomorrow and tell you what I can. Put you in the picture a bit.'

I NEED A FAVOUR

Angie answered the door to the Detective Sergeant wearing a short summer dress that was quite low cut and she was clearly not wearing a bra.

'Come in John. Sorry, I must look a state, I didn't sleep much last night.'

'Me too, it was a late one last night.'

They sat on the sofa together. John felt uncomfortable being so close to the woman he had lusted after since they met recently, even though he had been pleasured sexually the night before.

'So, what can you tell me?'

'Terry was charged last night with 2 charges of conspiracy to murder. This morning he had a private meeting with his lawyer and the procurator fiscal called a petition. He will then appear again in a week or so's time and the fiscal will decide if the charges go to trial or not.'

Angie leaned forward giving John a better view of her breasts. He didn't know if it was deliberate, but suspected it was.

'Will he go to trial, do you think?'

'It depends on a lot of things. The first charge, I don't know how to tell you this, conspiracy to murder your mother, he has admitted it.'

'What? Really, the bastard. Well, if he expects me to be waiting for him when he gets out of jail he is in for a shock. I won't be here; I will sell the house and move away. Where is he now, then?'

'The fiscal was quite clever that way. He is in Bowhouse prison outside Kilmarnock, the other guy, Colin Allardyce is in Barlinnie in Glasgow, so they should not be able to contact each other to compare stories.'

'Will I be able to visit?'

'Sure. You will need to contact them first, it's not really something I know about.'

'What if I took paperwork in with me, will he be able to sign it?'

'I would think that would be okay, but as I said, just ask on the phone. Why, what do you want him to sign?'

'I cannot stay here, God, it will be like living in a goldfish bowl. There is the woman whose husband got her mother killed. I want him to sign the rights of the house to me so that I can sell it.

'Do you think he will do that?'

'Yes, I have a plan for that.'

'There is also a second charge, also conspiracy to murder, this time it's for you.'

Angie's mouth fell open. She looked like somebody suffering a palsy for a moment but eventually got her voice back.

'Me. No way. He wanted be killed.'

'Yes, I am afraid so. The guy we intercepted on Tuesday night was, we think, coming here to kill you.'

'Is this all for real?'

'I am afraid so.'

'So, who is this other guy?'

'He is a Kilwinning man, Colin Allardyce. Terry met him on the train on the way home from a night out in Glasgow. He has confessed to being in your mother's house the night she died but says she had a heart attack.'

'I can't believe this. It's like a bad Netflix film. So, if the guy was supposed to kill my mum, what was Terry supposed to do?'

'According to him he was supposed to sort his pensions out for him.'

Angie laughed. 'My mother's life was worth about 30 quids worth of Terry's time. No, that doesn't make sense to me.'

'Nor me. Turns out he started having an affair with the guy's wife.'

'Who, my Terry? Having an affair. No, no, not him. Anyway, I would have known if he was up to something like that.'

'According to both of them it's been going on for a few weeks. Are you sure there was nothing different, has he had his usual sex drive?'

'No, that's why I am surprised. He hasn't been wanting it because the last few times we did it he hasn't been able to, you know, finish.'

'Wow. Must leave you frustrated.'

'You better believe it. But, there again we are both getting older, don't need it as much.'

'Do you think I could help?'

After saying it, he just looked at her.

'You mean you are after the reward I offered.'

John continued looking but said nothing else.

Angie looked straight into his eyes.

'John, I am ever so grateful, you saved my life.'

John expected a but.

'You certainly deserve a reward. When do you want to collect it?'

'What about Friday afternoon?'

'I was thinking more of you spending the night. Can you not make an excuse and stay the whole night with me?'

John swallowed hard, that was more than he expected. Wow, he thought.

'Right, of course. What about next Tuesday, if I come round about seven. Bring a bottle of something nice and bubbly.'

The Tuesday night would be ideal for him, he could tell Karen he needed to do nightshift on the Tuesday night killer's case.

'Sounds dreamy. However, there is a wee thing I need from you.'

John's mind was temporarily scrambles and the thought of what she was offering, that had his mind racing.

'Sorry, what?'

'Can you give me the address for Terry's lover. I would like to visit her and share our experiences.'

'I have it in my notebook in my car. It's outside.'

'Right, I will walk you out.'

They walked over slowly as Angie walked at the cop's pace.

When they reached the car John stopped.

'You know, really I shouldn't be giving you this information.'

When he looked at her, Angie fluttered her eyes at him and subtly leaned her boobs toward him.

'Seeing it's you,' he said, swallowing hard as he popped open his car's boot.

His coat was inside, and he reached into the pocket for his notebook.

Angie looked past him and saw his old truncheon on the floor of the boot. Suddenly an idea popped into her head, it would be ideal.

'John, since Terry was arrested I haven't felt safe in the house myself. Could I borrow your old truncheon? I wouldn't use it, but it would make me feel safer.'

John picked up the truncheon and looked at it.

'You know, I forgot it was in here. Take it but only use it as a deterrent. Don't want to have to arrest you.'

Angie took it and slipped it beneath her arm.

'Okay, until Tuesday then.'

'Eh, John, you were going to give me the address. Terry's lover.'

Even saying those last 2 words left a bitter taste in her mouth.

'Oh, right.'

He took a pen out and scribbled an address down.

'You didn't get this from me.'

'Thanks, see you Tuesday, I am looking forward to it,' Angie said, then walked away before he could reply.

GO TO JAIL, DIRECTLY TO JAIL

Bowhouse HMP, Kilmarnock. The number of times Angie drove past and saw the name on the signpost, never did she imagine she would be walking into the place one day. At least it wasn't far to drive, going to Glasgow would have been worse.

Angie sat in her car trying to prepare herself mentally to go inside. If that wasn't bad enough she was going to have to face her husband for the first time since she found out he was complicit in her mother's death.

'Deep breath, girl,' she said, then lifted the paperwork from the passenger seat and got out.

Security was a lot tighter than she thought it would be. At one stage she actually thought they would do an internal on her. Still, needs must, she kept thinking.

Terry was sitting waiting on her when she walked in. He looked up and smiled at her. A false foxy smile played on her lips for a second, all she could bear when she looked at him.

'Ang, I've been so stupid. But, you have to believe me, it was for your own good.'

'My own good?'

'I found out your mother had cancer.'

Angie gritted her teeth. It was bad enough everything he had done but trying to justify it by saying he did it for her was really lower than she thought he would sink.

'Colin, a guy I met, offered to ease her pain.'

Angie clenched her fists beneath the table, it was harder than she ever imagined, to sit and listen to him lying through his teeth to her. She knew he found out from her in the funeral car, that was the reason for the tears at the graveside.

'What about this woman you have been seeing?' she said in little more than a whisper, her mouth and throat suddenly dry.

'She, she came on to me. I was flattered but I couldn't manage it.'

There were tears appearing in his eyes. She wondered where he was hiding the onion.

'Angie, you are the only person I have ever loved.'

Angie reached a hand over and touched his. Her hand was shaking slightly.

'You are the only person I ever loved too.'

She was being honest, he was the only person she had loved, she didn't love him now.

'I have some good news. I contacted Douglas Forsyth Q.C., he is willing to take you as a client.'

'Forsyth, he gets everybody off. He really will represent me; I could get off?'

'Not Scot-free. Because you confessed you will be found guilty, but you know his reputation, he will get you off with a smack on the wrist.'

'How much will it cost?'

'A lot, but that doesn't matter as long as you get out of prison. We will need to sell the house, but I need to move anyway.'

'Sell the house? Will it cost that much?'

'It will cost a lot, but you need to know everybody is talking about me but not talking to me. The woman whose husband is a jailbird.'

'I'm sorry.'

'I've been to the lawyer. If you sign these papers and we can sell and free up the money we need.'

Terry signed without even looking at the paperwork. Now she could sell the house and transfer all the money to her new bank account. Sucker.

A buzzer sounded, time to go. All around women were crying as they said goodbye to their loved ones. Angie smiled across the table at Terry then left, joining the throng of weepy women. She was the only one laughing.

HELLO SADIE

Tuesday afternoon and strangely Angie felt incredibly calm. It would be a big twelve hours or so, but she wanted to just enjoy it.

A few days before she checked through Terry's clothes and found some of his old gear that would fit her. A tracksuit fitted, something she wouldn't be seen dead in, and trainers, Adidas Samba, that fitted with four pairs of socks on. Then she adjusted one of his baseball caps to make it fit with her hair tucked in it. From the garage she got her father's old walking stick. She knew one day it would come in handy.

Looking in the mirror she was, she hoped, unrecognizable. Lifting John's truncheon from her bed she slapped it into the palm of her hand.

'Showtime,' she said with a big smile.

Angie knew it was the right address because she recognised the slut's car in the drive. Personal plate which resembled her name, should be SLUT1 Ang thought to herself, laughing.

She had parked far round the corner in her friend's car she had borrowed, then walked round with a stoop and using the stick, disguising her usual gait completely. Even if she was spotted there was practically no chance of being recognised.

Carefully she slipped past the side of the car and down the side of the house. The back gate squeaked when she started to open it, so she opened it in slow motion to stop the noise.

There was one step up to the back door and Angie quickly calculated where she would need to aim, how high she would need to swing. The truncheon fitted snugly in the palm of her left hand. Being right-handed this would flummox investigating experts who looked at the injury she was about to inflict.

She was going to enjoy this, she thought with a smile. She knocked firmly on the back door and waited expectantly.

Behind her she heard the door open.

'Hello,' Sadie said, her last word.

Angie turned, as she did so she swung the policeman's baton up, aiming for her foe's head. It hit with a sickening thud that sent a shudder down her arm.

Angie had pivoted and lunged forward with such force she nearly landed on the stricken figure that had fallen like a dead weight. She got her balance back then looked down at her handywork.

Bullseye, she had cracked Sadie on the temple with a force that knocked her out and almost certainly killed her outright. There was no bleeding, but it was clear by the indent on her skull where she had connected.

Sadie's legs juddered then stopped but where she lay her legs were stopping the door from closing so Angie quickly pulled them back.

'Serves you right, bitch,' she said, before closing the door behind her and walking away. One thing was for sire, if she did live there was no way she could identify her.

Angie then carefully prowled through the house, looking for the woman's handbag. She found it beside the sofa. Carefully she opened it and lifted her purse out.

Opening it she found forty pounds in notes and a collection of bank and credit cards, exactly what she wanted. She pulled the notes out then stuffed the purse down the front of her tracksuit pants and retraced her steps back through to the back door.

She checked her bastarding husband's lover again, no sign of life, she thought with a smile, as she left the house and bent into her stoop again and headed back to the car.

Angie headed to Kilwinning town centre and parked up in the car park behind it. She sat in the car waiting for the right people. Junkies, preferably a couple. Maybe her plan hit a problem, the junkies would have got their methadone in the morning and probably were resting in the afternoon.

Just as she was about to give up a couple appeared and were walking from the direction of the car park through one of the lanes to the town centre.

She got out and walked quickly, catching up easily as they staggered along.

'Excuse me hen, you dropped your purse?'

The lassie turned with barely seeing eyes.

'No, it's not mine,' she said.

Her man, obviously a bit more compus, quickly jumped in.

'Oh, aye, it's yours. It's the one o bought you for your birthday.'

Angie handed it over and smiled. She had taken the cash out, they would need to use it to get cash.

Angie only a couple of hours left to get herself ready for the Detective Sergeant's arrival. When she got back from Kilwinning she slipped into her garage and stripped off all the clothes she had worn for the assault. They were deposited in two plastic bags which were dropped on the back seat of her car, along with the truncheon that had been wiped of any trace of DNA.

She took her friend's car back then retrieved her own, she had parked it in a car park in town but told her friend it was in the local garage getting fixed.

She was glad to finally get back home where she had a long, hot soak in the bath, washing any trace of guilt from her body. What she couldn't lose was the elation that she had committed, she hoped, the perfect murder.

After bathing, she put on her sexiest clothes, red basque, black suspenders and stockings with a pair of specially purchased crotchless pants.

She had only dressed like this once for her husband, but the affect wasn't what she planned, he suffered an embarrassing premature event, the opposite of his latest problem.

Hopefully the body she knew he craved wouldn't be too much for her visitor in her sexy get up.

Angie heard the copper's arrival before she saw him, the diesel engine of his taxi rattling outside like an old tractor.

Angie stood behind the front door and opened it when he knocked. She let him walk past before closing the door.

John turned and held out a bottle of Moet, wet with condensation.

'I have something for you,' he said as he proffered it.

Angie opened her silky white gown, showing her sexy underclothes.

'I have something for you too.'

John's hand shook slightly at the sight. For a moment the wet bottle nearly slipped from his grasp.

Angie leaned forward and took it from him before planting a wet kiss on him.

'Let's get that opened.'

Angie woke at four o'clock. John lay naked, sleeping beside her. He wasn't snoring but breathing noisily. Angie smiled; he deserved his rest after their session. John wasn't selfish in bed like her husband, he made sure she was satisfied, and she definitely was.

She walked over and sat at the window, watching as raindrops hit the windowpane and ran down it. In the street beyond it was quiet, save for the occasional car or two passing, probably people going to work. Who else would be up at that time unless they had to, she thought?

Her neighbour's homes were all in darkness. They were all curtain twitchers, getting their share of gossip from the number of police cars that had been at her house in the past while.

For once though, she wouldn't be the topic of conversation. Unless, of course, they saw her taking John back to the police station in the morning.

She couldn't believe the weather; the second of August and it was bucketing down outside. This was the height of summer, and the weather was absolute shit.

John turned and lay on his back, making his breathing even noisier. There was no way she was getting back to sleep soon with that racket, that was a certainty.

Lying on his back naked as he was, she could see his now flaccid cock lying invitingly. It was bigger than her husbands and he certainly knew how to use it. As she wondered when she would next have sex, with her marriage now effectively over, she decided she should avail of the facility again.

She had discarded the sexy underwear at different places around the house, from the lounge, up the stairs and the rest thrown on the bedroom floor. What she slept in was a light nightie. Taking it off, she threw it on the floor with the rest of her discarded clothes.

John woke with a start. Firstly, he struggled a bit to remember where he was in the strange surroundings but as the pleasurable sensations swept through him he soon realised where he was, and what Angie was after.

He smiled, it was the nicest way he had been woken from his sleep, ever.

They sat at the breakfast bar with coffee and croissants.

'Are you okay to drive me to the station? I could get a taxi.'

'No way. You shouldn't have to pay for your pleasure.'

'Well, we will need to go shortly. It was hard enough getting Karen to believe I was needed nightshift but if I am late home she will be suspicious.'

'It's only ten minutes to Irvine.'

'Irvine? I am based in Saltcoats. Have been for over 10 years now. We won't do that in ten minutes from Troon.'

'Oh, well, there were a couple of bags of clothes I want to drop off at the Tesco's recycling in Irvine.'

'Well, it's only a wee detour, we can do that.'

Angie stopped at the recycling bins while John got out and helpfully put the two bags of clothes in the chute.

'Bye, bye evidence,' Angie said to herself with a smile as she watched them drop out of sight.

John closed the back door and opened the passenger door again to get in.

'Did you lift your truncheon?'

'No, I didn't see it.'

'It was there beside the bags.'

He got back out and reached along the back seat until he found it.

'What's wrong, do you not need it now?'

'No. To tell you the truth, I don't think I could hit anybody if they broke in anyway. Anyway, I am going to get a burglar alarm fitted.'

'Do you know the best thing you could get? One of those ring doorbells.'

'That's the one I saw advertised on the telly. Right, I will get one in my new place.'

'Are you moving house?'

'Yes.'

Next time Angie stopped the car after the diversion to the bins was round the corner from the Saltcoats police station.

'What can I say? Last night was amazing.'

'I offered you a reward and you earned it.'

John reached over and put his hand on Angie's which was resting on the gearstick. Angie quickly pulled it away.

'I take it this is goodbye.'

'Goodbye, farewell. This was always going to be a one-off. You are married and I don't want any baggage like that.'

'What will you do now?'

'Well, I can't stay in Troon. I will always be the woman whose husband helped kill her mother. No, I think I will sell up and move away from the area altogether.'

'Well, it's goodbye then,' John said then leaned in for a kiss.

Angie leaned in towards him but turned her head and let him kiss her cheek.

John closed the door behind him and walked away.

Angie put the car in gear, released the handbrake and prepared to drive off.

IT'S NOT OVER UNTIL IT'S OVER

John Rose was disturbed from his sleep by his work phone ringing. He reached over automatically and grabbed it off the bedside cabinet.

'Rose.'

'Sir, Helen Begg. Sorry to disturb your day off but the Inspector said I should call. We have another murder, seems Colin Allardyce might have been telling the truth and the Ralston woman was a one-off. Looks like the Tuesday night killer has struck again, and he is in Barlinnie.'

'That's certainly an alibi. Do we know the victim?'

'Yes. Sadie Allardyce, Colin's wife.'

'Wow, this will really have the shit hitting the fan. The Inspector will be going choleric.'

'Yes, he must have had poker up his arse, and a red hot one at that.'

'Thought he would have liked that.'

'No comment on that. There is a muster at 13:00, he wants you there.'

'It's my day off. Are you sure he doesn't want me there.'

'No, he was insistent you have to be there.'

'Okay, see you then.'

Karen was in the living room, watching This Morning when he got up.

'You are up early.'

'Work phoned; I need to go in.'

'What? You were nightshift last night.'

'There's been another murder and it's connected to the case I have been on.'

'What, the case about our Angie's mother?'

'Well, the guy that did it, it's his wife, so it must be connected.'

'Are you not tired?'

'No, the adrenalin has got me going. I have a muster at 13:00.'

'Muster?'

'It's modern speak for a meeting.'

The Incident room was buzzing. There were at least a dozen detectives and Helen. She caught John's eye and he walked over to speak to her.

Since they had sex the week before she had been a bit doe-eyed whenever they met. John didn't want to burst her bubble, but she was the worst ride he probably ever had. Just lay there emotionless, letting him have his pleasure. Especially compared to Angie that night and this morning, she knew what a man wanted and gave him it.

'Hi John. Walker has taken over the investigation. He had been a bigger prick than ever, if that's possible,' she said quietly to him.

The Incident room closed firmly, and the hubbub silenced.

Inspector Kevin Walker walked over officiously to the new, bigger whiteboard.

'Ladies and gents, thanks for attending. We have another murder. Sadie Allardyce was found this morning by a neighbour. It would appear she opened the back door to her assailant and was struck once on the head by a blunt instrument. It would be easy to imagine it is connected to the previous case we are working.'

He raised a hand and waved it to John and Helen's small whiteboard.

'However, we must investigate it with an open mind. Now, with it being so warm due to this mini heatwave it has been harder for the pathologist to give us an accurate time of death. It could be any time from 2 o'clock yesterday afternoon until 8 o'clock last night. Remember that when you are doing door-to door.'

John shook his head as he watched most of the detectives' writing notes in their black books. Jesus, he thought, if they need to write small details like that they would be writing all day.

Walker turned to John and must have seen him shaking his head because he got a nasty look.

'D.S. Rose and P.C. Begg will cover the search of the house. The rest will carry out door-to door enquiries. The area has been divided up into sections and your names are on the map here. Remember the time frame and if anybody saw anything or were driving in the area ask them to check their dash cam in case there are any vehicles they don't recognise.'

Much as John Rose had expected the street map of the area around the Allardyce residence was colour co-ordinated with each pair of detectives given a different colour. He felt like saying pretty maps don't solve crime but that was for another day.

There was a bit of noise again as the detectives talked as they looked to see who they were paired with and who they were matched with.

'Before you go, I have already had the press on wanting information, so we need results and fast. I have been told the mobile incident unit will in the area at 3 o'clock, so I want results by then. Okay, let's get out there and find the killer.'

Helen was back on driving duties as they headed to Kilwinning.

As they drove out of the secure compound John spoke first.

'Walker must like you.'

'What makes you think that?'

'Searching the house is one of the most important jobs after a murder has been committed.'

'Maybe he likes you.'

'I can assure you he doesn't. Tolerates is as far as it goes. If I dropped dead tomorrow he wouldn't shed a tear. No, he must want you to go in there and I am the makeshift in the deal.'

After that the conversation was limited after their tryst the week before.

As she parked up outside the Allardyce's next door neighbours house, they were just taking the body out from the house in a body bag, on a stretcher.

They got out of the car and stood head bowed as the body was slipped into a waiting Transit van.

'Round the back,' he said as he went in the direction the body had been brought.

The forensic team were finishing off. John didn't know the lead guy's name but knew him to nod too.

'Anything new? The Inspector didn't give us much.'

'For good reason, there isn't much. The lady was struck a single blow to the temple from a blunt instrument. No sign of the weapon, no fingerprints, a partial footprint that might be significant. I would guess a size 8 and looking from the cast I would stick my neck out and say an old Adidas samba trainer.'

'Could it not belong to some-one else? Window cleaner, anybody like that?'

The guy shrugged.

'Was she wearing jewellery, wedding bands or anything else?'

'Yes, she had a small gold necklace and 3 rings on her ring finger. The footprint is practically all we have from the house. If you find anything else give us a shout.'

Although they had been in the house before, there was a distinctly strange feeling in the house, one that neither John nor Helen had liked.

'What are we looking for first?' John asked his trainee.

'The weapon.'

'That would be a Brucey bonus. No, chances are he took the weapon with him.'

'Who says it is a man?'

'Helen, when we have a murder case the perpetrator is always supposed to be a man until we know different. It's not sexist or anything like that, just one of the few traditions we are still allowed.'

'Well, we want her handbag, see if anythings missing,' Helen then said, excitedly.

'Correct. Has it been a robbery or is it linked to the Tuesday night murders? Remember, no preconceived ideas.'

'Well, with suspect in Barlinnie and the other in Bowhouse there's 2 suspects off the list.'

'Maybe, but one of them could have arranged it. If you want a directory of thugs, murderers and assassins, where better to be.'

'Never thought of that.'

The walked into the living room. Her handbag was at the side of the sofa. John put a gloved hand inside and found tissues, lipstick and a paper mask. No purse or other valuables.

'Not there. Where else would you keep your purse?'

'In a drawer. Could be anywhere really.'

Helen started checking the drawers on the living room display cabinet and any other nooks in the lounge.

'I've got her mobile phone. We will need to get this to the phone guru,' John said, as he slipped it in an evidence bag and wrote the details on it.

For the next hour they checked every imaginable place where her purse could be but found nothing.

'It looks like it's been a robbery gone wrong,' John said. 'Best we get back to headquarters and try to trace her bank cards. You can get the pleasure of phoning Inspector Walker the news.'

Next morning and D.S. John Rose was trying to trace the missing bank cards but felt like he was banging his head against a very hard place.

With new banking regulations in place, they were having to jump through hoops to find out who Sadie Allardyce banked with and the last time she had used any of her cards.

Eventually they got a call from Virgin bank saying the card had been used the previous evening at the local Co-op in Kilwinning town centre.

'Let's go, see if they have CCTV or if anybody remembers seeing them,' John said, pleased their enquiry had taken a leap forward.

Helen smiled at the last comment, it wasn't a corner shop it was a supermarket. Okay, it wasn't in a large town or city but it would still be a very busy shop. John probably didn't get involved in the weekly shop, she mused.

The duty manager in the Co-op looked surprised when John showed her his warrant card. Uniforms she was used to, junkies would steal anything for money for a fix but this seemed a level above.

'Do you have CCTV covering the tills?'

'Not yet. We've been promised it within the year.'

'Well, that could be handy if we don't catch the culprit before then.'

Helen looked away so the store manager didn't see her snigger. She thought his sarcasm was funny at times.

'Right, we are trying to trace a stolen bank card used in here last night around 18:30.'

He pulled a scrap of paper from his pocket and read from it.

'The sum of £82.45 was spent and paid for contactless.'

'I know the 2 you mean. Junkies or alkies, I can't tell the difference, but there was a couple in here about that time. Out their trumpets, she was worse than him, could hardly walk. Usually buy 1 or 2 items. Last night they had a trolley full.'

'Do you remember what they bought?'

'Usual, only more. Basket filled with vodka and steaks.'

'They eat well for junkies,' Helen interjected.

The store manager looked at her as if she was stupid.

'The steaks are to sell for a quick buck.'

Helen felt her face go a bit red but didn't reply.

'When are you working until tonight?' John asked.

'I am working backshift all week; we are open until 10 o'clock and I will be here until after that.'

'I assume they haven't used the card today so they might be out tonight. If they do call 999 straight away and say I said they were to be arrested.'

'Could you give Helen a full description of them, we will need to do the same with the Tesco store down the street.'

'Sure.'

They walked down the street heading for the small Tesco's at the other end of the High Street. As they passed the square a couple of space cadets emerged from one of the alleyways which lead through from the car parks.

'Jesus, I hope none of those 2 have been driving,' John said, then looked at Helen.

'That's them,' she said, 'God, they are even wearing the same clothes.'

'Let's follow them, bet they are off to the Co-op again.'

He was right. This time they got a trolley, gave them something to hold on to because they were so drunk or stoned they were wobbling down the street.

Helen picked up a basket and followed while John spoke to the manager, warned her of her latest customers. Then he phoned for uniforms to assist if they got out of hand.

When they appeared back at the till area the manager confirmed Helen had been correct, they were the same 2 from the night before.

Two uniforms appeared outside, John stepped forward and motioned through the window for them to wait outside for the moment.

John walked up and held the trolley as they approached the self-service area, stopping them in their tracks. His police i.d. was on a chain round his neck and he showed it.

The guy looked up through half shut eyes. He was definitely under the influence of drink or drugs but wasn't totally out of it. The woman was in the same state but needed the trolley to keep her steady.

'Excuse me sir, how are you paying?

'By card. It's the safest way,' he said, then tried to wink, failing badly.

'Safest way,' the woman parroted, speaking slurrily.

'Would you mind, can I see your bank card.'

'Sure,' the guy said, then fumbled in his pockets. 'It's in her name,' he added, pointing to his beau.

'Her name,' she said, smiling and pointing to herself.

John took the card with gloved hands, read the owner's name before dropping it in an evidence bag.

'Sadie Allardyce, is that you?'

The woman waved a thumb unsteadily, 'that's me.'

'You are looking well for a dead woman. There again, maybe you are not.'

John signalled out to the uniforms, and they made their way in.

'Would you mind accompanying these gents to the police station.'

'What? It is her card. Tell them Sarah.'

'It's says Sadie on the card.'

'Yes, that's right, Sadie. That's her.'

'Her.'

'No, it's not. Where did you get the bank card?' Helen interjected.

'We found it,' the guy said.

'Where?'

'A woman gave us it,' the woman said, suddenly realising they could be in bother.

'Shut up Mary.'

'Mary? I thought it was Sadie.'

'Okay, gents, let's take them out,' John said to the uniforms who were standing behind them waiting.

The two plods took one each and guided them out to their van parked down the street a bit. Helen produced 2 large evidence bags from her handbag, and they followed to empty the junkies of their possessions before they were put in the van.

The only significant thing they found was a purse in the women's shoulder bag that had more of Sadie Allardyce's membership cards.

'Right, let's get them off to Saltcoats nick. We will see you there, officers.'

Helen drove the car out of the car park and was excited at their find and capture.

'We've got them John. The Inspector will be cock a hoop.'

'Helen, there is no way on this Earth they did it. Christ they would be lucky to tie their own shoelaces, no way could they have clubbed some-one to death.'

'I still think I should phone the Inspector.'

John shook his head, exasperated.

'Tell you what, I will get him on hands free, you can do the talking.'

Before waiting for a reply, he had the number ringing.

'Walker.'

'Hi Sir, it's Helen Begg here. I am with D.S. Rose. We have apprehended a couple who have been using Sadie Allardyce's bank card.'

'What? Really!'

'Yes sir.'

'We've got them already. Brilliant work Helen.'

'Thanks sir.'

'I will see you when you get back,' he said then ended the call abruptly.

John shook his head again.

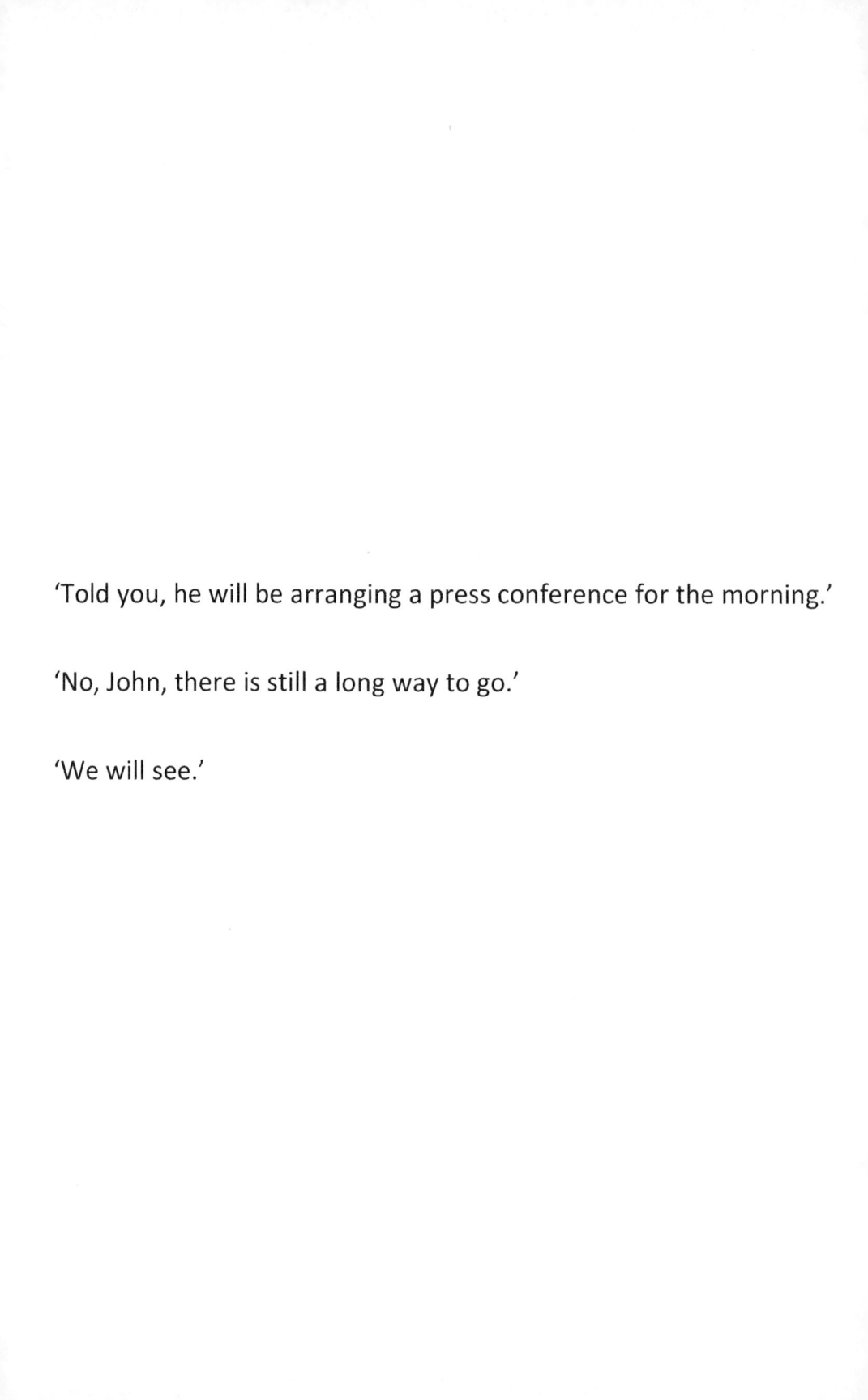

'Told you, he will be arranging a press conference for the morning.'

'No, John, there is still a long way to go.'

'We will see.'

END OF A BEAUTIFUL PARTNERSHIP

John's phone rang at 07:33, Helen's name lit up on the screen.

'We've got them. Kevin wants you to attend the press conference at 9 o'clock with us.'

She was speaking quickly and excitedly.

'Slow down, what are you talking about?'

'The two we apprehended last night have confessed to the killing.'

'What, no way? Do you believe them? Really?'

'Yes. I was here during the night and was with them when they owned up to it.'

'I thought we agreed to go home and interview them this morning when they were sober or junk free or whatever.'

'Yes, I went home but Kevin phoned and asked me to come in and help him with the interview.'

'Helen, I think you have been very naïve, there is no way those two junkies could have robbed and killed Sadie Allardyce, I would stake my pension on it. The state they were in she could have pushed them over.'

'Kevin says when drug addicted folk have taken drugs they can be very strong.'

'Kevin, Kevin, Kevin. You can tell your precious Kevin I will have a word with him when I get in.'

John then cut the call.

Detective Inspector Kevin Walker was in his office, checking his looks in his mobile phone. John Rose opened his office door quietly and walked in without being invited. W

When he closed the door the D.I. turned with a start, surprised to find someone else in his office, uninvited.

'Oh, John, I take it you heard the good news,' his clipped voice full of pride.

'No, I heard you had arrested 2 people but there is no way they carried out any murder.'

'John, they confessed.'

'Detective Inspector, you are about to carry out the biggest miscarriage of justice since Lee Harvey Oswald was blamed for killing JFK.'

'They confessed, gave details about the murder nobody else knew, John, they did it.'

'What did you promise them, a fix if they signed the confessions.'

'Detective Sergeant, I don't like your attitude, however, as you are leading up the investigation I expect you to be there.'

'I won't be at the charade you are planning; I intend to carry on looking for the real killer.'

'No, you won't. If you do not attend the conference you will be off the case and back to your office looking at cold cases.'

'Cold cases it is,' he said as he barged out and threw the door closed behind him.

Helen was in the incident room. She was dressed in a navy-blue business suit.

'What's he offered? A promotion to detective?'

'What are you talking about?'

'Your new friend Kevin couldn't get a confession from those 2 without doing something underhand.'

Helen's silence showed her guilt.

'Hope you 2 will be happy together.'

John turned and started walking out of the room but turned at the threshold and walked back. He stood close so that anyone entering the room couldn't hear their conversation.

'I need a favour. I think after our time together you owe me something or you would have been staying in uniform for a lot longer.'

'What?'

'I am back on cold cases, but I want to solve this murder. Will you go through the door-to-door interviews and pass on anything they found?.'

Helen took his hand.

'I will do but I am afraid we can't have sex again.'

'I understand and thanks,' John said, trying to sound contrite.

COLD, COLD, HOT!

John Rose sat in his office, watching the news conference on the BBC iplayer. The D.I. pompous as ever and Helen providing the eye candy.

John wished he was playing buzzword bingo, Walker was giving an utter gobshite speech with almost every word being a buzzword. Acted expeditedly, threw major resources, no stone unturned,

He couldn't watch it and switched it and the computer off.

Instead, he got a blank piece of paper and wrote on in in block capitals, who, where, when, why and how. Apart from the who did it and when, the main thing was why. That seemed the key to this investigation.

Was Sadie a smoking gun? Could she give evidence that would sink either her husband Colin, or her lover Terry?

Could Angie have been after revenge and got somebody to beat her up and maybe they went too far.

An hour later he was disturbed by a gentle knock on his office door.

Helen handed him a bulging folder, a copy of all the papers we wanted. She never spoke, just turned and left.

'Thanks,' he said after her, but she never acknowledged him.

John's phone buzzed. It was Karen, wanting him to bring fish and chips home for tea. That meant he hadn't to be late that night. When he saw the time on his phone he was shocked, it was 14:10. He had been engrossed in the reports. He only had one left, it said the same as a few of the others and added the note: old guy in a tracksuit, walking stick, limp.

Possibly a red herring but there were also a good number of no contacts. They would be working and best knocked up at night. Not that night, he was under orders.

Next day John worked backshift. He had drawn up a list of the people he wanted to revisit and the homes where they didn't get anyone in.

The first door he tried was at the top of the road from the Allardyce's house. The old man had passed the house in the late afternoon, they reckoned. How could an old man with a walking stick, supposedly shambling down the street, have the strength to deliver a one-strike blow that could kill somebody, he wondered.

It was a disguise, had to be. This was no opportunistic robbery; it was a hit. The more he thought about it the more he was convinced of that.

As he was leaving a car was pulling into the next door's drive. It was one of the no contacts, John swooped before they could get in the house.

He showed his i.d. and introduced himself.

The couple were thirty-somethings, designer clothes, sunglasses, bleached teeth and tanned, either from sunbeds or bottles.

'Excuse me, I take it you know about Sadie Allardyce's death on Tuesday.'

The woman moved her sunglasses down a bit to look at him.

'Oh, the old woman. Sadie. Was that her name? We have never met, we only moved in 2 years ago.'

Years ago, John would have been surprised that you didn't know everyone in your neighbourhood. The Allardyces lived across the road and 4 doors down, not exactly the opposite end of the estate.

'What I want to know is if you saw anything or anybody on Tuesday afternoon or evening? Strangers in the area, a car or van you hadn't seen before?'

'Sorry,' the woman said, without even thinking about it.

'Hold on,' the guy said. 'There was a Fiat Panda parked round the corner. An old black one, it was. I thinking something didn't add up about it at the time. Don't remember what.'

'Darren is into cars,' the woman said, as if to endorse his information.

Darren smiled. 'I have an old Spitfire in the garage,' he said proudly.

'What about the registration?'

Darren clicked his fingers. 'That was it. It was an old plate on a newish car, but it didn't look like a personal plate.'

'You don't remember any of the plate? It could be important. Very important.'

'I can check my dashcam.'

John suddenly felt excited, this could be key.

Darren unlocked his car and unclipped the dashcam camera.

'Just need to connect it to the laptop.'

They walked into the house together.

'We have just finished decorating the lounge,' the woman said proudly.

John put on a false smile; he thought it looked gross. It was all decorated in black and white. Then he remembered where he had seen similar, at Ma Kelly's house.

He broke into a huge smile at the thought of the 2 houses, one in a private estate and the other in a council one both decorated horribly. He wondered what Darren's wife would think of the notion of her and Ma Kelly having the same taste.

'Would you like a drink?', the woman asked, while Darren busied himself at the dining table on the laptop.

'No thanks, not while I am on duty.'

'They do it on films and T.V.,' she said.

John smiled at her naiveite.

'Was the woman really old? We heard it was a heart attack or stroke, something like that.'

'We are waiting for the results back of the autopsy,' he said, not wanting to alarm her if she hadn't heard anything else.

'Here it is,' Darren said.

On the clip Darren was approaching the car and had to wait as an old Volvo slowly passed the Fiat.

'It's amazing how clear these pictures are,' John said.

The car was a Fiat and John wrote the registration down.

'No sign of the driver?'

Darren's car then passed the parked car and drove round the corner and into his drive. The street was empty, nobody in sight.

'This could be very helpful,' John said before getting out of the house as quick as he could, the monochrome décor was annoying his senses.

GREENOCK?

John sat at his computer the next morning and desperately put the registration number into the computer, this could be the big break he needed.

The door-to-door had only thrown up 2 things, an old guy with a slight stoop and a walking stick and the Fiat Panda. If they tied up he had his killer.

The owner of the Fiat was a Frank O'Riley and his address was in Greenock. Greenock? He ran his name through the computer, but he came out clean. If he was a hit man, and a good one, he would have been clean.

There was only one thing he could do, road trip. A 30-mile trip up the coast. It was a nice morning, what could be better. Until he arrived, of course.

The sat nav took him to a run-down looking council area. The kind of place where a dog with 3 legs and 1 eye was called Lucky. When he drew up at the house he was in luck, the car was in the driveway.

John got out and looked at it before knocking the front door. Something about it didn't match to the car he had seen in the dash-cam video. It was an old car although it was a black Fiat Panda.

Before he could knock on the door it opened and an irate Frank O'Riley walked out to face him. He was over 6 foot tall and stood straight as a poker.

'What are you after?'

'Sorry to bother you. I am Detective Sergeant John Rose. Your car was reported in an RTA in Kilwinning on Tuesday night. Can you account for your actions on Tuesday night?'

'Don't recognise you, you aren't from Greenock.'

The guy was smarter than he looked and obviously knew the police. Surprising for somebody who didn't have a record.

'No, I am from North Ayrshire?'

'Long way to come for a road traffic accident?'

The guy was also street wise, best not bullshit, John thought.

'Okay, I am investigating a murder and a car with your number plate was flagged up in the area on the night of the murder.'

'Me, a murder suspect,' Frank said, before laughing loudly. 'The guys at the station will crack up at that one.'

'You aren't a police officer are you?'

'No, I am a cleaner. I clean the main Greenock police station. Tuesday night my car was in the station car park.'

John laughed along with Frank, only because he knew he had been outsmarted.

'Well, the bad news my friend is that somebody has got a copy of your plates and has put them on another car. You could now be you get speeding tickets from Ayrshire or maybe they will steal petrol and drive off.'

The smile slipped off his face, it suddenly wasn't funny.

'What can I do?'

'Next time you are at work tell the desk sergeant, he will note it and put it on record.'

'Right, thanks,' the guy said.

John drove back down the coast, struggling to put this piece of the jigsaw into the right place. He was sure the car was relevant, more so now he found out it was a ringer of some sort.

He didn't drive straight to the station but instead made a detour back to Kilwinning and the Allardyce's house. Parking the car outside the house he walked back to where the car had been parked.

On the way there and back he was looking for CCTV or a Ring doorbell, anything that would have given him an image of this "old man". He had a feeling that the old man with the strange walk was a disguise, a bit like Colin's hi-viz, being invisible in broad daylight.

He sat back in his car, frustrated, but the frustration just made him more determined.

John sat at the dining table and rubbed his stomach; he was full to the ginnels. Karen had dished up his favourite dinner, steak pie with potatoes and peas and carrots. It was probably the first time they had been able to sit down like that since he started on the Tuesday night killer case.

'Did you know cousin Angie was selling up?'

'She did mention she had to move away. Could you imagine her situation, all her neighbours talking about her? A celebrity in the neighbourhood for all the wrong reasons.'

'She has a lovely house; I was looking at it on the net today on my phone. Do you want to get your laptop out so I can see the pictures bigger?'

John got his laptop out and they sat on the sofa together.

When he brought the website up the house wasn't listed.

'She must have sold it already. Go back and click on houses under offer.'

John looked at Karen without speaking. He was the detective, he knew how to get information like that.

The familiar image of the front of the Carpenter's house was there with "under offer" written under it.

'Wow, can you imagine an ex-local house selling for £180,000 pounds, that's more than ours is worth.'

'Well, it is in Troon.'

He slowly flicked through the pictures. The front of the house, the hallway, the open plan lounge and kitchen. The settee where they had kissed and fondled. The upstairs hall, the main bedroom. The bedroom looked different in daylight, he had only seen it in the dark or by the light of one of the bedside lamps.

Still, the memory of that night had blood rushing to his groin. What he would give for a repeat of that night.

'Right, move on,' Karen said.

John had not realised he had been daydreaming and moved on to the spare bedroom then the bathroom.

Next it was outside.

'Wow, the back door is something else. When you are retired you can get ours like that.'

Karen wasn't kidding, it was all laid out on different levels with neat brickwork and beds full of colourful planting.

'I don't think I could ever get our place looking like that.'

The next pictures were of the outside of the garage then the inside.

'Imagine that, an empty garage. Well, it's not exactly empty, but what is there is tidy.'

John's attention was caught but not by that. On the opposite wall was a collection of number plates.

Karen noticed John was daydreaming again.

'Why do you think they have all those number plates?' he said, speaking to himself.

Karen answered.

'Because unlike you they have personal plates on their cars, have done for years. Those will be the original ones from their cars.'

'Oh, right,' he said, listening but not really hearing.

'The thing is, there are 2 missing.'

Karen looked at the display and saw he was right, there was a gap in one of the rows where 2 plates had clearly been removed.

KNEW YOU WOULD ROUND TO SEE ME

Angie opened the front door and found John Rose standing.

'On your own are you?'' she said as she looked past him to check.

'Yes, just me. Have you not got Terry's car back from the pound yet? They must be finished with it by now?'

In the large driveway her Aygo sat alone.

'Yes, I got it, sold it.'

'House sold too I see.'

'Yes, cash buyer for a quick sale. Out of here next week. Anyway, I knew you would be round to see me.'

'Oh, why was that?'

'Because you were a good detective, I knew that from the first time I met you. Something about your demeanour told me there was something different about you. Different but in a good way.'

'I will take that as a compliment.'

'Yes, it was meant as one. So, what do we take care of first, business or pleasure?'

'If we are dealing with both, then pleasure first, of course. Don't think that would be the same after we discuss business.'

Angie leaned forward and kissed him, which he responded to.

She took him by the hand and lead him up the stairs to the bedroom.

This time, after they stripped off, a more sedate manner from the last time when clothes were ripped off in anticipation.

Angie was naked first and lay on top of the bed.

John joined her and started the session by kissing and then nibbling each nipple in turn. His hand then went between her legs. This time it was hectic, not meant to arouse or pleasure her but ready her to take him. When he felt she was set to take him he entered her.

The sex was unsophisticated, he plundered her. Pounding as hard and fast as he could, it wasn't for her pleasure her this time but to let her know who was the in control, who had the power between them.

Afterwards they lay on the bed, the only noise was the heavy breathing from both as they tried to get their breathing patterns back to normal.

'So, business, then. Why did you do it?'

'Why? You need to ask why? I will tell you something although you probably already know most of it. Karen and I were, like you, were born and brought up in the 60's and 70's. We didn't have much but neither did anybody else, so we weren't different. Although we didn't have stuff, we had rules and the first rule we had was you don't nick anybody's boyfriend.'

'Is that any different from us being here?'

'This was a business arrangement. I knew the first time we met you were desperate to have me. Don't deny it.'

'I won't. The thing is, if it hadn't been for the old number plates you used I wouldn't have solved it, I was stumped. You nearly committed the prefect murder.'

Angie leaned up on her arm and faced him. He kept looking at the ceiling.

'Don't you get it; you were meant to solve it.'

John leaned up on his arm now and faced her.

'Why?'

'So that you could lose or bury the evidence. After all, you were incriminated.'

'Why, because we ended up in bed? Might ruin my marriage but hardly a crime.'

'Come on, surely you are smarter than that. Right, here I am a wee housewife. Who is going to believe I had the brains and brawn to murder somebody? I would need somebody to help me plan it. That would be you. You told me where she lived, you told me to use somebody else's car and to take on a disguise and then you gave me the murder weapon. If you get your truncheon checked for DNA you will no doubt find some of that woman's skin cells on it.'

Even then she couldn't bring herself to say Sadie's name.

'I took a risk using my friends Panda that was much newer than my old one but it was a calculated risk.'

'How did you know your old car was still on the road?'

'Easy. Well, I could say you told me but all I had to do was put the details in one of those car buying sites. When they gave me a value I knew it was still on the road.'

'Very clever.'

'I knew you would put 2 and 2 together and check back on the DVLA to see who previously owned the car.'

'Actually, I guessed it was you before checking. Karen showed me the pictures of your house on the estate agent's page. and it was obvious there were 2 number plates missing from your collection.'

'Then, on the evening after I killed her, we went to bed. Celebrating our evil deed. Next morning, we went to Irvine, and you dumped the clothes I wore in the recycling bins.'

'You really have thought of everything.'

'Yes. If I go down, you come with me. So, to keep us out of jail you will need to bury the evidence you found.'

John was dressed and stood with Angie in her hallway.

'So, where will you go?'

'You know Terry was right after all. It's too cold here most of the year and the summers are too short. I am heading to Portugal. I might just rent at first, I might buy something eventually.'

'What about us? Is this it over?'

'Not necessarily, you could come out to Portugal and visit. I will make you more than welcome.'

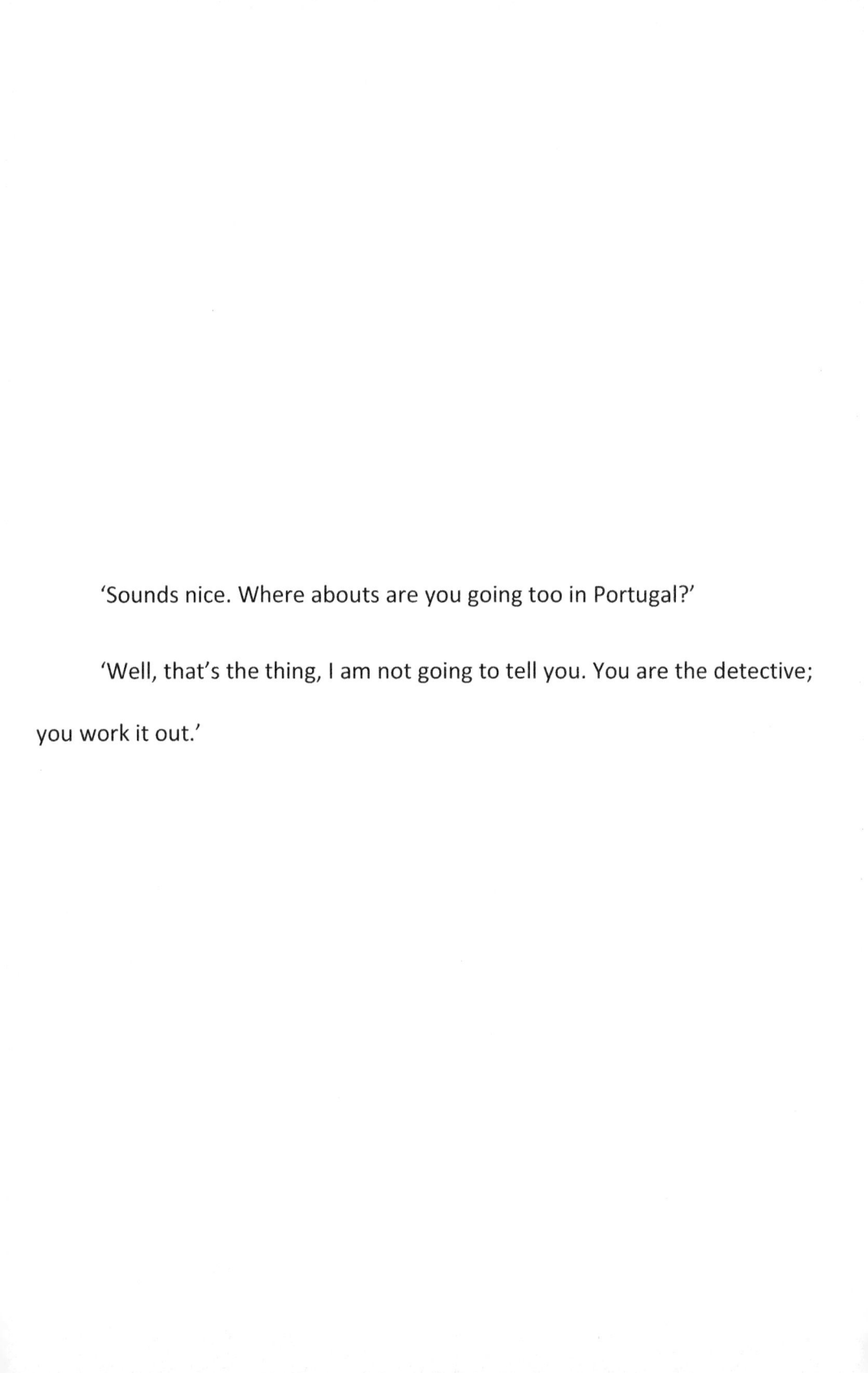

'Sounds nice. Where abouts are you going too in Portugal?'

'Well, that's the thing, I am not going to tell you. You are the detective; you work it out.'

Printed in Great Britain
by Amazon